ARLENE McFARLANE

Murder, Curlers & Kegs

A Valentine Beaumont
Mini Mystery

ISBN-13: 978-0-9953076-7-4

Published by ParadiseDeer Publishing
Canada

Cover Art by Sue Traynor
Formatting by Author E.M.S.

Acknowledgments

Enormous cheers to my smart team: my editor ~ Karen Dale Harris, proofreader ~ Noël Kristan Higgins, formatter ~ Amy Atwell, and cover artist ~ Sue Traynor. You've been an absolute dream to work with.

Sisterly hugs and deepest appreciation to *New York Times* and *USA Today* bestselling author Darynda Jones. You're the greatest, and your stunning endorsement has made me smile.

Warmest gratitude to my friend, Paul Courtney. You make the best bread in the world! Thank you for being my technical advisor on bread machines.

As always, it's with a grateful heart when I think of you, my dedicated reader. This journey has been an amazing one because of you!

My cherished family: your love and encouragement has meant everything to me. I love you beyond the stars and back.

Finally, thank you, God. Keep leading the way!

To every talented beautician:

If anyone can relate to the words in the Murder, Curlers series,

it's you!

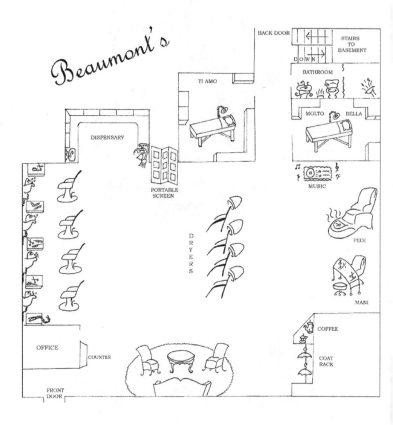

Beaumont's

BACK DOOR

STAIRS
TO
BASEMENT

DOWN

BATHROOM

TI AMO

MOLTO   BELLA

DISPENSARY

MUSIC

PORTABLE
SCREEN

PEDI

D
R
Y
E
R
S

MANI

COFFEE

OFFICE

COUNTER

COAT
RACK

FRONT
DOOR

Chapter 1

My name is Valentine Beaumont. When I was a kid, I dreamed of being a beautician. It was either that or becoming a movie star, the kind who wore sparkly gowns and lots of diamonds. But since acting wasn't in my blood, the movie-star dream died a fast death.

In the end, I became a licensed aesthetician and hairstylist, and I opened Beaumont's, my Mediterranean-themed salon, in the heart of Rueland, Massachusetts. Some days I even glitzed up my outfits. Not to movie-star proportions, but enough to give me pleasure without looking cuckoo.

I currently have three employees. Two are talented beyond measure. The third is inept beyond hope.

Though cutting hair is my main profession, I've also solved the odd crime. Some would say *solved* is too generous a term, but there were naysayers everywhere. And when it came down to it, I was still using my beauty tools…just in a more creative way.

It was Sunday morning, and I hurried out of the cold November wind, stomping my feet to warm up in my friend Jimmy O'Shea's new, soon-to-be-opened restaurant.

Jimmy and I had been friends since he'd moved here from California in the ninth grade. He was a surfer and a first-class ticket scalper and had often blessed us with cut-rate Bruins, Celtics, and Red Sox tickets. But he'd come into some money, thanks to a rich, deceased aunt, and had swapped selling tickets for buying a favorite local eatery that had been on the market for a month. The favorite eatery, the Wee Irish Goat, had undergone changes and had now become the Wee Irish Dude. *Dude* was the language Jimmy spoke.

Since Beaumont's was closed on Sundays and Mondays, my staff and I had agreed to help Jimmy finish unloading boxes, set beer kegs into place, and clean both floors of the restaurant before his grand opening Saturday.

I was going to miss seeing Gene Kelly and dozens of other actors' pictures plastered on the walls. But the dartboards, beer kegs, ceiling fans, wall plaques of all things Irish, and the Celtic welcome sign with a greeting I'd never pronounce in a million years gave the place a true Irish-pub feel, and I was convinced the Wee Irish Dude would be a success in its own right.

I set my ever-present black beauty bag on a table and took off my tailored leather jacket. I was attempting to tame my hair from the nasty weather when I spotted Phyllis—my inept-beyond-hope employee—bent over Jimmy at the far end of the bar. On the wall, behind Phyllis's head, was an Irish saying that read *If it's drowning you're after, don't torment yourself with shallow water.*

I grimaced at the sign, wondering if anyone had ever posed the sentiment after meeting Phyllis. And what was she doing anyway?

She was in a fuzzy black-and-yellow striped sweater, and it looked like she was smearing black gunk on Jimmy's brows and lashes. And Jimmy, in his green Celtics jersey and cape over his shoulders, was angled back taking it.

I didn't want to ask Phyllis what was up. I'd had my own hellish morning, and this was low on the list of things I cared to know about.

Max thumped a box on the bar and paraded over to me. "What happened to *you*? You're late. And what's that in your eye?"

Max was my righthand man in the salon and nosy friend outside the salon. Nothing got by him, and his clever remarks said as much. If there were a Pulitzer Prize for excellence in being a smartass, Max would win the award hands down.

I whipped a long burgundy strand of hair off my forehead, gave up in frustration at taming it, and blinked at Max. "I poked my eye with my mascara wand this morning. Why?"

He leaned his handsome, boyish face in until he was an inch from my nose. "Your eye's all red."

"You should've seen it earlier." I pushed him back. "And my morning only got better after that."

"I sense sarcasm."

A sigh escaped me in exasperation. "Seems someone's playing a nasty joke on me."

He rubbed his hands together, his hazel eyes mischievously glinting more green than brown. "If it's nasty, I want to hear about it."

"Figured you would." I glanced around the room, then centered on Max. "Sitting straight up on my porch this morning was a dildo with a perm rod fastened around the bottom. No note. No explanation."

Max scrunched up his nose. "What kind of a sick joke is that?"

I studied him carefully. "I don't know, but I'd feel better knowing you didn't have any part of it."

He planted his hands on his hips. "Lovey, I may be a lot of things, but I draw the line at playing sick pranks." He pursed his lips as if he were thinking. "Maybe one of Mr. Long Arm of the Law's cops is behind it."

This was Max's playful term for Michael Romero, an extremely sexy, ruggedly handsome, tough police detective I'd fallen for months ago during a past murder case in my salon. After a series of mishaps and misunderstandings, we'd officially just started dating, most recently, a night out bowling.

"Aren't Rueland's finest always teasing you about catching that crook using a perm rod?"

"Don't forget *and wrapping it around his family jewels*!" I griped.

"I was being polite."

Oh brother. "I don't know why any cop would get that personal. This feels different."

"Speaking of feeling different…" He gestured to the far end of the bar at Phyllis. "What's going on with Madame Medusa lately? She's been all keen about hair and stuff."

Max comparing Phyllis to one of Disney's villains spoke volumes about their relationship. "She didn't tell you? Phyllis has been taking a course on haircutting and eyelash and eyebrow tinting."

I glanced over at my incompetent employee, suddenly realizing the latter was what she was attempting on Jimmy. I had to give her credit. At least she was trying to improve her skills.

Max gaped at her in disbelief, and I couldn't be sure if he was impressed with this news, or if he'd finally thought he'd heard it all.

Before he could utter another word, Jimmy cried, "Riiiiighteous!"

Phyllis whipped off Jimmy's cape, a smile of accomplishment on her face.

Jimmy was lovingly referred to as the Skink because of his short neck, long torso, and short legs. On top of that, he had curly bleached-blond hair that corkscrewed out in every direction. Now that Phyllis was done with him, his thick brows and blond eyelashes were black. He looked like Groucho Marx without the bushy mustache and fat cigar.

My jaw dropped a foot, and I blinked in shock.

"Hey, dudette!" He wagged his shaggy eyebrows at me. "Sexy, huh?"

I closed my mouth and swallowed. "That's one word for it."

"You know they say Armenian women and Irish men are the world's sexiest people. Want to make it world's sexiest couple and get it on?"

I knew of the survey he was talking about. "I'm saving myself for marriage."

"Then let's get married!"

You had to admire Jimmy. He saw himself as a stud. Unfortunately, he was the only one.

"There's also a little French running through my blood, and Ukrain—"

He was so pumped he cut me off. "So we'll have a massage à toi."

"You mean a *ménage à trois*. And I don't think that'd work in this case."

"*I'm* willing to make it work. Max?" He waggled his brows in Max's direction. "What do you think of the new look?"

"I think you got what you paid for."

"I didn't pay a thing."

Max brightened. "Then you should be pleased."

Jimmy looked at himself in the mirror behind the bar. "I am, dude. Like far *out*! Always willing to try something new. And since Phyllis has been helping with the restaurant, the Skink's happy to assist with her training."

"Maybe you could also assist with her wardrobe," Max muttered.

And it only took my presence to start the insults. Thing was, Phyllis wasn't merely a poor stylist, she was also a seamstress in the worst degree. But in an uncanny way, her outfits actually suited her.

"Hello, ding-dong." Phyllis eyed Max. "I'm standing right here."

"Oh. I thought you flew off to make honey."

Phyllis almost tripped over the cape she was holding, hurrying to get in Max's face. "Just because I'm wearing black-and-yellow stripes, you're saying *what*? I look like a bumblebee?"

"No, you look more like a hippo pretending to be a bumblebee."

"I'll hippo *you*!" Phyllis's mahogany curls shook as she raised her fist in Max's face.

Max swatted her hand away, unconcerned, but Phyllis was on a roll.

"I know everyone around here hates me. Just because I'm not skinny like Valentine or have natural talent like *some* people."

Max gave a small shrug. "Weight and talent have nothing to do with it. We'd hate you anyway."

"Max!" I gawked at him.

"Okay!" he conceded, palms up. "We don't hate you, Phyllis."

"Hmph," Phyllis said smugly.

"We just don't like you very much."

I rolled my eyes so far to the back of my head I could almost see the tag on my top.

The other thing about Phyllis was she was distantly related on my mother's side. So distant, in fact, nobody could figure out where the bloodline came in. In my mind, Phyllis was the mangy dog nobody wanted, and she was sort of adopted into the family. If truth be told, it was something I preferred not to share. Seemed Phyllis was okay with this arrangement as well.

"You'll see," Phyllis snapped. "Once I master this course, I'll get a job anywhere I please."

"Why wait?" Max asked. "Handsome Groomers is hiring."

Phyllis squinted meanly at him. "*That* place is for *dogs*."

"What's your point?"

Jock, my last—but certainly not least—employee, appeared at the top of the curved staircase, hands on hips, a dozen big brown wooden barrels behind him. "Am I the only one working around here?"

I gazed up at the gorgeous mocha-skinned face of this Argentinean Hercules and all but forgot about the arguing duo in front of me, not to mention my red eye, messy hair, and the dildo delivery.

"Sleeping Beauty arrives." Jock winked at me, holding the stare longer than necessary.

Any remaining chill in my bones vacated my body, and a wave of heat rushed through me from the remark. His way of reminding me how I'd woken up tangled in his arms a few short weeks ago when the whole staff cruised the Bahamas.

I knew better than to say anything on the matter. Instead, I tightened my lips, snatched a nearby cloth, and wiped down a table. I caught his grin, but he left it alone. For now. That was another thing about Jock. There was always a later.

"Jimmy," he said, a trace of humor left in his deep, sensual voice, "what's in these big kegs?"

Jimmy ambled to the bottom of the stairs and looked up at Jock. "Like, they're empty, dude. Since the small kegs at the bar hide those ugly beer canisters, I thought it'd be cool to complete the rustic look by lining the wide steps with those big kahunas." He blinked through his black lashes. "You know, like one barrel on each step."

Jock nodded. "Max, I'd like your help, please."

Max charged up the steps. "At your service."

Jock motioned to the barrels. "We're going to rotate these down one step at a time. Got it? I'll do the first one. You grab the next keg."

"Aye-aye, cap-i-tan!"

Everyone else got busy cleaning, and a moment later we heard a heavy thud. "Look out!" Max squealed.

Jimmy, Phyllis, and I jerked our heads toward the stairs and watched a barrel bounce down the wooden steps. Jock secured two drums against the railing so they wouldn't get knocked down in the process.

"I couldn't hold on!" Max cried from the top of the landing. "It was too heavy."

The keg swerved off the last two steps, went thumpity-thump, and crashed on the floor in front of us. Cartoon-like, the sides split open, and at once we knew why the barrel was too heavy. It contained a dead body. And the victim looked like Jimmy.

Chapter 2

"Dooley!" Jimmy cried, gaping down at the slight, curled-up form in the busted keg.

We all looked down at the curly-haired Jimmy look-alike. Apart from a neat hole through his bloody skull, and blond eyebrows instead of black, he was a replica of the Skink.

"You know this guy?" Jock had jogged down the stairs and was standing beside Jimmy.

"Yeah, dude." Jimmy winced. "Like, Dooley's my first cousin."

"How the heck did he wind up dead in a wooden barrel?" Phyllis asked.

Jimmy shrugged, the world on his shoulders. "Beats me, dudette."

"Did he…um, shoot himself?" Max held back a breath like he didn't want to know the answer to that.

Jock examined the broken drum. "No gun in sight."

Max let out a *whew* that it wasn't suicide, though it didn't make anything better. We all took a few moments to offer Jimmy condolences and regain composure. Except Jock. He was dialing the police.

"How'd your cousin even get in the restaurant?" Max asked.

"Fair question, dude." Jimmy's black eyebrows creased into a frown. "Dooley was going to be my cook."

He exhaled, looking off into the distance. "When we were kids, Dools loved playing chef. He was always in the kitchen, creating a huge meatball sub or homemade onion rings or chocolate mousse cake." His gaze swung back to us. "He'd moved to New York as a teen but came back and was here last night, working on the menus. Said he'd shut everything off when he was done. So I locked the door behind me, played a few hands of poker with some buddies, then went home." He hung his head and rubbed his face, holding back the emotions. "I should've stayed, man. Dooley was the best cousin I had, and I wasn't here for him."

I controlled the nausea in my stomach at seeing another corpse and wrapped my arm around his shoulder. "I'm sorry, Jimmy. Sounds like you were close. He even looked like you."

Max and Phyllis agreed, muttering similar remarks.

"Well, I'm out of here." Phyllis backed up to the door. "Nothing like another murder to put a kink in your day."

I grabbed her by the arm. "You can't go anywhere. The police will want a statement from all of us."

"I need to get to my course," she argued. "We're learning how to tint eyebrows and eyelashes today."

Max gaped from Jimmy's Groucho Marx eyebrows back to Phyllis. "You mean you did *that* to Jimmy, and you hadn't learned how?"

Phyllis nodded. "They told us to practice over the weekend to get a feel for the tint. Who else was I going to work on?"

Max stared down at the corpse, and I knew he was thinking the dead would be Phyllis's best bet.

"Sorry, Phyllis," I said. "You'll have to wait until the police get here."

"And it's Sunday," Max declared. "What kind of beauty class is taught on a Sunday?"

Phyllis crossed her arms. "With everyone working during regular business hours, nights and Sundays were the only times they could run the course. Look it up if you don't believe me."

"I don't need to. If you're enrolled, I already know it's a horse and donkey show."

An exasperated sigh left my lips. "Don't you mean dog and pony show?"

"No." He let that sit like *horse and donkey* was self-explanatory.

Jimmy fell to his knees in front of Dooley's lifeless body and shook his head. "I had a feeling something was bothering Dools." He peered up at me. "He had a habit of chewing his nails when he was stressed. And like, look at them. Stubs."

Max leaned in, then straightened. "His cuticles don't look so good either."

I sliced Max a terse look.

Tamping down my queasy stomach, I knelt beside Jimmy. "What was bothering him?"

Jimmy shook his head, long and slow. "I don't know, but I think it had to do with his time in prison."

"*Prison!*" I lurched to my feet, dropping my cloth in surprise.

Jimmy swiped it off the floor and stood beside me. "Like, I know. Shocker, right? But I thought it was all good. Dools had served his time for auto theft, and he was getting on with his life."

"Then what was worrying him?"

"I think it was more a *who* than a *what*." He plunked the cloth in my hand. "Some woman had called here a couple of times to speak to him. And when Dools hung up the phone, he was clearly agitated."

I bit my bottom lip. "Maybe it was a girlfriend or a relative."

"Nope. No girlfriend to speak of, and if it'd been family, he would've told me."

I was deliberating on this when the sound of sirens wailed down the street, and a sense that this was about to explode came over me.

Within seconds, Rueland's finest hustled through Jimmy's front door. Romero led the pack in a black leather jacket, jeans, and a plaid flannel shirt. His dark hair was ruffled from the wind, his full mouth unsmiling and controlled. His gait was slow, bordering on painful, thanks to yours truly dropping a pretty, marbleized bowling ball on his foot a few days ago. Accidentally, of course.

The heat I felt a few moments ago from Jock skyrocketed at the sight of Romero. Tall, dark, and handsome didn't nearly describe the sensuality that exuded from this hard-muscled, Mediterranean-skinned, tough cop.

Romero caught my eye, gave me a private nod that sent a shiver down to my groin, then called out orders to his men. Instantly, the place turned into a scene from *CSI*. Crime scene tape went up, fingerprint kits popped open, and cameras started clicking.

I swallowed, admiring the way Romero took charge of a situation, then quickly straightened at the silent look he transferred from the dead body to me. I stepped back out of the way and wrung the cloth in my hands, interpreting the look as you're-in-deep-doo-doo.

Though I'd known Romero for five months and was familiar with his personality, the dangerous stares he could give either made me hot and sweaty or made me want to run for cover.

In this case I told myself I had nothing to fear. I mean, there were four other witnesses here today. On top of which, I'd never even met Dooley. How could I be responsible for this? Anyway, I had my own issues to worry about.

Topping the list, this morning's dildo-and-perm-rod delivery. Gut instinct said this wasn't a joke. But who would go to such lengths to freak me out? An old boyfriend? Ha! It'd been so long since I'd had one of those, I couldn't even recall the last one's name.

Get serious. Who else?

Candace Needlemeyer, my archenemy from beauty school? Hmm. I wouldn't put anything past Candace. She was Maleficent, Cruella de Vil, and the Wicked Queen from *Snow White* rolled into one. And even those villains' nastiness didn't hold a candle to Candace's antics.

Candace had opened Supremo Stylists three blocks from Beaumont's a month after I'd opened the salon and had used every trick in the book to rob business from me. She'd even attempted to steal my staff, centering on Max, and then Jock. I'd once offered her Phyllis, but I guess Candace didn't want too much of a good thing.

I puffed air out my nose in frustration. If I never saw Candace again, it'd be too soon. Yet hard as it was, I tried to think rationally where she was concerned. No doubt she riled me, but I had a tough time seeing her pull a prank this low. Scary and crazy wasn't her style. She'd played dirty often enough and proved she'd stop at nothing to undermine me. But this wasn't wrecking a mannequin in beauty school or ruining a color job or telling lies about me. This felt different.

Think, think, think. Who else could've done something so vile?

I rolled my gaze over to Phyllis, shifting my thoughts from one crazy broad to another. I pressed my lips together and stifled a moan. I didn't suspect Phyllis of any wrongdoing, but she'd left a long trail of unhappy customers. What if one of those clients thought it was time to get even for her screw-ups?

This wasn't such a bizarre thought. True, I'd never been sued—praise the Lord—but people had a funny way of dealing with things. Perhaps someone was playing vigilante, taking the law into his or her own hands to seek justice for a crime committed in Phyllis's chair. One could argue that what she did to her clients day-to-day *was a crime*.

I mentally turned back the clock to Phyllis's more spectacular disasters, the list too long to go through. But as with everything where Phyllis was involved, certain things stood out.

What if it was the woman who resembled Alice Cooper after Phyllis's makeover? Or the client who stamped out of the shop with a crater-sized hole in the back of her hair?

Or the lady who fled after Phyllis tweezed off all her eyebrows?

The list was endless. It'd take a lifetime to figure out which client could've done this, if indeed it were a client. But were any of these people crazy enough to resort to such an outlandish prank? Were they not satisfied with the follow-up apology and promised discount for the next salon service? Did any of them even know about my history with the perm-rod debacle?

The more I thought about the likelihood of a customer placing a dildo on my porch, the more holes I found in this theory. Sure, Phyllis was unpopular with clients, and a good many never returned to her chair, but I couldn't see a true connection from a disgruntled customer to something as personal—and directed at me—as a dildo delivery.

I cracked a knuckle, ruminating on this, when I spotted Romero bending over Dooley. He took notes, then conferred with Jock.

I gulped, not sure what I thought about this new bond between the two men. Romero was a macho, hard-headed Italian. Jock was ex-navy and a master-at-arms. I hadn't given myself to Romero intimately, but I had a feeling if he ever found out I'd woken up in Jock's bed—naked—well, I wasn't sure how helpful Jock's decorated past would be. I choked back the trepidation at what could happen if I ever let that one-time occurrence slip from my mouth.

Jock said something to Romero, and Romero gave me the eye. A second later, he sauntered over, caution marking his steps.

I bumped back against the table I'd just cleaned and put on an innocent smile though my insides were a jumbled mess of nerves.

"How are you doing?" he asked casually, as if it'd been weeks since I'd last seen him instead of a few days, and we weren't standing in the middle of a crime scene.

I gave him a wary look, the small scar on his cheekbone adding to how threatening he appeared. "Fine?" I held back a nervous nose twitch. "And you?"

No sense bringing up his hurt foot…again. Besides, the mishap never would've happened if he hadn't been putting on the moves while teaching me the finer points of bowling. *Show-off.*

He did a so-so tilt with his head. "Seems we've got a situation." He looked over his shoulder at the victim, then back at me.

If I'd had a challenge-free morning, I wouldn't have felt myself stiffen. But it *hadn't* been challenge-free. My morning had been complete with the dildo delivery, my sore eye, unruly hair, Phyllis's butchery, plus, discovering poor Jimmy's dead cousin. And Romero's borderline accusatory look fired me up in all the wrong ways.

I smacked the cloth on the table and crossed my arms, everything coming to a mountainous head. "Why don't you just say it?"

"Say what?"

"Something sarcastic about me discovering another dead body."

He gave a slight shrug. "I'm actually getting used to it." He looked from my irritated eye to my disheveled hair, then swept me in for a hug. "You okay?"

Not expecting this tender reaction from him, I let my defenses down. "Mmm-hmm." I melted in his arms, controlling the tears from rolling down my face.

His muscular hands held my head close to his chest. His Iron Man watch rested against my cheek. "Jock told me what happened. Anything you want to add?"

I stayed curled up for a bit, luxuriating in the comforting scent of his Arctic Spruce and the smooth feel of his watch. Telling myself I couldn't stay this way forever, I backed up and wiped my nose. "Did you know about Dooley's incarceration?"

"Yep. Dooley was well known. He was a misguided kid, easily led. But he did his time. Been out for a couple of months now."

I thought about this. "Jimmy felt there was something about Dooley's time behind bars that was bothering him."

"Such as?"

"I don't know. But there was a woman involved who'd called him at the restaurant."

"We'll look into it," he said. "By the way, I don't want to scare you, but Ziggy Stoaks escaped from Rivers View Correctional Center last night."

"Ziggy Stoaks?" I repeated, eyebrows raised.

"Yeah." Romero looked at me quizzically. "You forgotten already? You helped put him away for murdering Max's friend Freddie." He paused. "You've been the butt of so many perm-rod jokes, I figured you wouldn't have forgotten that historic day."

I hadn't. That day had changed my life. I'd gone from an unknown beautician of a mediocre salon to Rueland's amateur beauty sleuth. Unwanted notoriety at its best.

"His buddy Luther Boyle wasn't with him," Romero added. "Probably nothing to worry about. But stay on the alert."

My heart pounded in my chest, which was where the color in my face felt like it had drained to, and a lump formed in my throat.

Romero took hold of me by both shoulders and gave me a shake. "What's wrong? You're white as a ghost."

In my mind, I was back to that day at the landfill, tripping over heaps of garbage in an effort to nab two murderers. Luther Boyle had been an easier catch. He'd tackled me first, but once I'd speared him in the gut with my metal tail comb, he'd passed out from the sight of blood.

Ziggy Stoaks was different. He wasn't as big as Boyle, and he had a limp, so I hadn't thought he'd get far. But he was crafty and put up a good fight. In all honesty, I'd been lucky to come out alive. Thank God for my beauty tools.

"Mikey," one of the uniforms called to Romero.

Romero waved a hand back at the cop, his focus still on my face. "What is it, Valentine? Say something."

I forced down the lump and stared up into his eyes. "I got a delivery this morning on my front porch."

"What kind of delivery?"

I lifted one shoulder in hesitation. "It wasn't flowers… and it wasn't exactly chocolates."

His mouth went hard. "What exactly *was* it?"

I lowered my gaze to the ground, embarrassed. "A dildo wrapped with a white perm rod."

He tilted my chin up with his finger. "Is this a joke?"

"I thought so at first, but with Ziggy escaping…and a white perm rod's what I used when I caught him—"

"Yeah." Romero quickly calculated the implications. "You're not staying alone till he's been apprehended."

"Pardon?" His concern was sweet, but I didn't like the bossy tone.

"You heard me. Call it a hunch, but it sounds like Stoaks hasn't forgiven you for turning him into a choir boy. And unless you can tell me anyone else you suspect of delivering that dildo on your doorstep, you're going to stay at my house."

I shook my head no. "You can take the thing and dust it for fingerprints. I didn't touch it. It's on my porch, top of the steps to the right."

"Fine." He called over one of his men, explained the situation, and the cop departed. Then Romero zeroed in on me again. "What are you doing here anyway?"

I stared over his shoulder at the Skink who was shaking his head, still in disbelief. "We were helping Jimmy get ready for his grand opening Saturday."

Romero nodded. "Until the ID unit's finished sweeping the scene, consider your jobs here done. And I'll repeat, you're going to stay at my place. I'll have one of my men escort you there."

"I can't. I have things to do."

"Such as?" He gave me a skeptical look, like he wondered if I'd forgotten my recent promise. The one where I was supposed to contemplate keeping my tools strictly for hair instead of catching crooks. Romero's way of saying, stay out of police investigations.

If he really wanted to know, I *had* contemplated keeping my tools strictly for hair. But I had no intention of locking myself away until Ziggy Stoaks was found. I'd captured him once. If I had to do it again, I would.

I bit the inside of my cheek. "I have to check in on a friend."

"What friend?"

"Sheesh." I rammed my hands on my hips. "Do you have to know everything?"

"When it comes to you, yes."

I huffed, acting like the victim when in truth I couldn't blame Romero for the third-degree questioning. I'd gotten in over my head too many times, but I'd learned from those past mistakes. Hadn't I?

I gazed back at the Skink. "As soon as we're free to go, I'm simply going to take Jimmy home. Make sure he's all right." Jimmy didn't know this, but the more I thought about it, the more I liked the idea.

Romero deliberated on my plan, still eyeing me like he didn't trust me. "Fine. I can't force you to come to my home. But to be safe," he added, "a cruiser will be patrolling your neighborhood for unusual activity."

"No need. Ray Donoochi's down the street. I'll fill him in on this morning's occurrence."

Ray was a cop for the Boston Police Department. I knew Romero had worked with him in the past. Ray was as tall as he was wide. He also had two teenage sons who were strong and who'd learned self-defense from their father. The Donoochis weren't my bodyguards, and they weren't automatic buffers against danger. Their failure to prevent the dildo delivery already proved that. Still, they were nearby if I needed them.

"Ray's a good man, but his wife's got to cut back on the desserts she's serving him." Romero gave me a stern look. "Don't go anywhere alone. You spot anything suspicious, call me. Hear?"

I saluted.

"Don't be a smartass." He took his finger and brushed a stray hair back off my forehead, his intense blue eyes darkening on mine. "Bowling may have been a disaster, but I have other things planned for you. I want you in one piece."

It was never easy distinguishing whether Romero's words were a warning or a guarantee. Nonetheless, I felt a stirring down low, taking this as a subtle reminder of a couple of steamy nights several weeks ago, cuddling in a private cabana on the beach in the Bahamas.

True, I'd woken up in Jock's arms a few days before that, and to the uninformed person, I probably sounded like a trollop. But there were extenuating factors to my night with Jock that justified my actions.

Romero flicked the tip of my nose, then glanced over his shoulder. "I'm needed over there. In the meantime, stay out of trouble." At that, he backed up and headed over to the cop who'd called him.

I breathed out a sigh of relief. I'd stay out of trouble all right. How I did that while finding a killer was another question.

Chapter 3

Once we'd each given a statement to the police, Phyllis tramped off to her course, Jock huddled in a group with the cops, and Max, Jimmy, and I stood there like stooges, not sure what to do next.

Since Jock had picked up Max this morning, and Phyllis had driven Jimmy in to get a head start on his new look, I suggested the three of us hop into my car and head to Jimmy's place. Wasn't that what I'd proposed to Romero?

We swung out of the restaurant's parking lot, Ziggy's escape forefront in my mind. Max and Jimmy prattled on about the murder and what the consequences would be for the Wee Irish Dude. Meanwhile, I steered onto Montgomery on the alert as advised by Romero. I looked both ways at every turn and constantly checked my rearview mirror in case someone was following me.

"Boy, dudette." Jimmy leaned forward in the backseat, bobbing his head from Max to me. "I've ridden in VWs before, but your yellow Bug is what a sorry dude like me needs to cheer him up."

"It really is Valentine, isn't it?" Max egged Jimmy on.

"And then some, dude." Jimmy nodded out the window. "The sun's even coming out. It must like Daisy Bug, too."

I cut Max a shrewd look at his shallow attempt to brighten the Skink's mood, then veered onto a cul-de-sac and asked Jimmy which house was his.

He pointed over my shoulder to the charming blue and yellow Cape Cod two-story sitting at the far end of the circle, looking like something out of *Better Homes and Gardens*. "Good ol' Aunt Neila," Jimmy said. "She could really do up a place right."

Max's eyes were big like saucers. "You're not kidding. You inherited this, too?"

"Like, did I ever. Moved in a few weeks ago."

Max nodded. "You going to live here by yourself?"

Jimmy shrugged, sadness setting in once again. "I was going to ask Dooley to move in with me. He had his own place, but it was in a rundown apartment building. And I thought it'd be kinda cool if we shared the house."

We moseyed through the front door, and it felt like good ol' Aunt Neila was still here. Everything looked so cheerful, from the delicate princess drapes to the tasteful knick-knacks. I almost expected to see a basket of fresh muffins on the kitchen counter.

"Hey, look!" Max pointed to an open pantry next to the kitchen. "A bread machine. Don't you love those things?"

Jimmy wandered over to it. "This was Dooley's. He brought a few things over that he didn't want to keep at his apartment. Even made us a few loaves. He was an expert at bread-making."

While Max was drooling over the machine, I scanned the place. "Did Dooley bring anything else over?"

"Sure, dudette. I'll show you the room I was going to set up for him." He led me down a hall into a neat, white-walled bedroom with blue accents and billowy lighthouse-patterned curtains. There was a TV and Polaroid camera sitting on a table, a bed opposite the table, and several boxes on the floor piled with cookbooks and loose papers.

"Like, what are you looking for?" Jimmy wanted to know.

I studied the room. "I'm not sure. Something that may explain what happened to Dooley."

"Far out, dudette! You're taking the *case*? You'll unearth who murdered Dooley?"

"Let's not jump the gun…so to speak. I'm merely… curious."

"Yeah, like I know what that means." Jimmy snorted. "First, you step your sexy high heels in the murder scene, all innocent-like, and then *whammo*!" He clapped his hands in the air, making me flinch. "Valentine Beaumont, super sleuth to the rescue."

Jimmy should've majored in drama. "Let's see how it goes, okay?" I knelt in front of the boxes on the floor.

"Ten four." He trotted to the door. "Like, righteous."

I rubbed my chin, mulling things over, then raised my eyes to Jimmy's back. "You said you were *going* to ask Dooley to move in, right?"

He turned from the door. "That's right."

"Then if you hadn't asked him yet, and if he had an apartment, why was he hauling things here?"

"Good question." He scratched his head, pondering this. "I wish I had a good answer. All he said was some stuff was important to him, and he didn't trust the rats at his place not to go through anything."

I looked back down at the boxes, thinking out loud. "Or maybe he didn't trust that *someone* wouldn't go through his things."

His eyes widened as if he hadn't considered this. "Yeah. Like, maybe he was onto whoever killed him." His eyes bugged out even more. "Maybe he knew who it was all along."

"It's possible." I gestured at the Polaroid. "Whose camera?"

"Also Dooley's. Since he got out of prison, he liked snapping pictures. Sort of a hobby. And Polaroids are super-popular again. We had one when I was a kid, but it was nothing like these new ones." He stared at the camera. "Dooley never let me see any photos, though. He was kinda private that way." He blinked down, his black lashes brushing his cheeks, his bushy brows giving a sad wiggle. "I wonder what he would've thought of my new look."

My heart went out to Jimmy, and I offered an encouraging smile. "I'm sure he would've thought it was... righteous."

"Yeah. Probs." He faltered at the doorframe, his head low. "I really appreciate this, dudette. Your hair's kinda witchy today, and your eye looks tortured, but hey, I won't hold that against you. If anyone can find Dooley's killer, *you* can."

I was touched by his backward vote of confidence. I just wished I felt the same way.

Jimmy stumbled back to the kitchen where Max was likely fawning over gadgets, and I went to work rummaging through the boxes on the bedroom floor.

Nothing much of anything caught my *tortured* eye or seemed significant. Cookbooks galore. Old bills. Receipts. Court documents. All stuff from four, five years ago.

I raked a snarled clump of hair behind my ear, leaned my elbow on one of the boxes, and raised a brow at the closet. Hmm. Was there anything in there that belonged to Dooley? Wouldn't hurt to have a look inside.

I worked the kinks out of my legs and ambled over to the closet. Inside, I found a hoodie and a fairly new leather jacket. Probably didn't want the rats to get at these either.

I did a quick search through the hoodie and found a pack of gum, a crumpled tissue, and a bit of loose change. Nothing noteworthy. I pushed it aside and felt around in the leather jacket's outer pockets. Nothing remarkable there either. I squeezed the fabric above the left pocket and felt something like a folded paper, or tickets, or maybe a wad of bills.

I took the jacket off the hanger, sat on the bed, and groped for an inner pocket. Aha. I undid the zipper and tugged out a white envelope bent in half. Inside the envelope was a small stack of 2" x 3" photos. I glanced at the Polaroid on the table, then back at the pictures, taking a moment to register what I was seeing.

The pictures were of me. All of them. A shot of me getting out of my car at the hospital where I played Mon Sac Est Ton Sac, a favorite made-up game with the sick kids. Another of me locking the back door after work. In the next shot, I was entering Friar Tuck's Donuts beside the salon.

My breath caught in my throat, and I tried not to shake, but I was trembling so hard the photos slipped through my fingers and fell onto the shiny hardwood floor.

I slid down amidst the pictures and took a deep breath, pulling myself together. I sorted through the stack, squinting closely at the first photo. I remembered that day at the hospital. In fact, it was last Monday when the kids giggled their time away, using the beauty items in my bag to make me beautiful, or "more bootiful" as one child had put it.

I stared at the photo of me getting out of my car, wearing the multi-colored sweater I'd bought at that new eclectic boutique in Burlington, Rueland's neighboring town. Okay. Not one of my smarter purchases.

I went through the pictures and could recall almost each place where they'd been taken and when. One about three and a half weeks ago after work when Max and I had treated ourselves to a couple of greasy fried-chicken dinners at Lick-a-Chick. Another of me playing Catwoman, digging around late one night outside Rueland Retirement. Wait. That was back in September during a previous murder case.

And what about this one? Taken last month after that case had ended. Romero and I had been testing the dating waters, and I was in a romantic stupor after we'd just exited the retirement home.

I kept flipping. Whoa. This one was only a few days ago. Me throwing a gutter-ball at Lucky Lanes. Likely before Romero had stepped in to demonstrate how it was done. The bowling alley was busy that night, and it'd never occurred to me I was being watched. But Dooley must've been in the back somewhere to take this shot.

A sharp prickle darted up my spine, and I fought to stay calm. Dooley had been photographing me for at least two months. I backtracked to Romero saying Dooley had been out of prison a few months now. But why had he begun stalking me? Did this have something to do with his incarceration?

According to Jimmy, Dooley had come back from New York to cook at the restaurant. So where did I enter the picture? Could Dooley have been the one who'd delivered the dildo, last night yet? Sounded like something a stalker might do. And who was the woman who'd called the restaurant and upset Dooley?

I briefly wondered if any of this was connected to Ziggy. But he'd been doing time at Rivers View, which was in Norfolt. And Dooley had been in New York. Two different states and miles apart. Plus, Ziggy's handprints were all over that dildo. I leaned against the bed, stumped.

I put the photos back in the envelope and gave a slight shiver. Like it or not, the pictures tied me to Dooley and put me smack in the middle of a murder investigation. I had to give these to Romero. Maybe he'd shed light on the puzzle.

Max and Jimmy's voices moved up the hall toward me. Before they even made it through the doorway, Max hoisted up the bread machine.

"Jimmy's giving me Dooley's bread maker. After all, Dooley's not going to need it anymore."

I blinked wide-eyed at Max at his insensitive comment.

"What!" He looked apologetically from me to Jimmy. "Oops, I mean Dooley won't be baking bread where he's going. Although it should be warm enough."

Oh Lord.

Thankfully, Jimmy was so easygoing he didn't take offense.

Max lowered the bread machine and for the first time actually looked at me on the floor with Dooley's leather jacket on my lap and the envelope full of pictures in my hand.

"What are you doing sprawled down there? Some new form of yoga?"

I got to my feet, flung the jacket on the bed, and showed them the photos.

"What are pictures of you doing in Dooley's jacket?" Jimmy asked. "Like, that's plain creepy."

"Tell me about it." Another shiver tore through my body.

"It's more than creepy. It's criminal." Max rested the machine on his hip and snatched a photo from my hand. "I told you he wouldn't be baking where he was going." He examined the picture closely. "Hey! This one's of you and me that day we went to Lick-a-Chick."

He gaped back up at me. "Why am *I* in the photo?" He dumped the bread maker on the bed and scoured through the rest of the shots. "Whew. Thank goodness that's the only one."

"Yes, thank goodness," I said. "Wouldn't want your life to be in danger, after all."

"Lovey," Max retorted, "you may be used to this *Criminal Minds* stuff, but some of us don't live life on the edge." He draped an arm around Jimmy's spindly shoulder. "Some of us are more delicate."

I glared at him. "Start using that bread machine you just inherited, and you're going to lose that delicate look of yours."

Max withdrew his arm from around Jimmy's shoulder and stuck out his lip in a pout.

"Jimmy," I said, my voice softening, "the police need to see these. Are you okay with me passing them on?"

"Whatever you think is best, dudette. Like, I trust you."

Max lugged the bread machine off the bed, then gave me a sour look. If a word bubble had been suspended over his head, it would've said *Killjoy*. He stared down at himself like he was weighing the prospects of what daily homemade bread would do to him.

Without ceremony, he handed the machine to Jimmy. "I guess I'll be better off without this."

"Hey, dude," Jimmy said, nodding, "you know where it is if you change your mind."

Max thanked him, gave me a haughty look, and sailed out of the room.

Chapter 4

Max and I piled into my car without exchanging a word. That was fine because I needed to talk to Romero.

I jerked out my phone while Max fidgeted with the clasp on his seatbelt. He turned to me, unable to stay quiet for long. "Do you really think I'd get out of hand if I had a bread machine?"

"They're killers," I replied flatly, calling Romero's cell number.

He chewed on that while I told Romero about the pictures I'd found in Dooley's coat pocket.

"You found *what?*" Romero shouted. "Where are you?"

"Just leaving Jimmy's house."

"May I ask how you found pictures in Dooley's coat pocket if you were at Jimmy's?"

I narrowed my eyes at the phone, not caring for his abrupt tone. "You may ask…if you ask nicely."

"I'm asking as nicely as I can." He bit off his words with deliberation, like he was controlling himself. "How do you find these things? And why pictures of *you?*"

"I found them because Dooley had a few things stored at Jimmy's. He had a coat hanging in Jimmy's closet, and I went through it. As for the pictures, I don't know why he had them."

He sighed. "We're at Dooley's apartment right now. Not much of anything here. Bunch of old cookbooks, pots and pans, worn furniture, business cards for the Wee Irish Dude." There was a moment's silence like he was thinking that last part over. "And he was going to be Chef Boyardee at the restaurant?"

"That's right."

"Well, there's no clue as to who offed him. And you finding pictures he took of you only complicates things."

"Hey, I wasn't too thrilled about it either. And if you want to know, you're also in one of the photos."

"Great. Hope he got my good side."

Romero had a bad side?

"Looks like we have a dead stalker on our hands," he concluded.

Neither one of us said anything to that, but the heavy exhale on the other end said he was frustrated. "How soon can you drop off the pictures at the station?"

"I'm on my way now. I'll be glad to be rid of them."

"Good. They can get a head start running them through the lab. I'm going back to the restaurant. The ID unit's still there. Probably be there all night."

I sensed there was more he wasn't saying, and experience told me I was out of luck if I started asking questions. But I couldn't ignore the fact that a murderer who hated me had escaped on the same day an ex-con who was stalking me was murdered. And what about the delivery on my porch? Romero was too good a detective not to see the coincidences. It was just like him to deliberately not share anything else on the subject.

I imagined him glancing at the glow-in-the-dark hands on his Iron Man watch, then heard plates clanking in the background. He said something to a cop about taking it easy with the dishware, then came back on the line. "Is Jimmy seriously naming the restaurant the Wee Irish Dude?"

"You have a better name in mind for a surfer-slash-scalper-turned-restaurateur?"

"How 'bout Jimmy's Cuckoo?"

I screwed up my nose, not that Romero could see it. "Doesn't have the same ring to it."

"Speaking of the restaurant, it's likely Dooley knew his killer. Maybe knew him well."

I pressed the phone closer to my ear. "What are you getting at?"

"No forced entry into the place. In Jimmy's preliminary statement, he said he locked up when he left the restaurant, then went to play poker with some buddies."

I added two and two together, uncomfortable with where this was heading. "Why does it sound like you suspect Jimmy?"

He let out an aggravated sigh. "You should know better than anyone, at this point we can't rule out anybody. And it's no secret that Jimmy inherited a shitload of money. From *their* aunt. They could've quarreled about this."

I was miffed. "You're wrong about Jimmy. He has a huge heart. Maybe he did inherit a lot of money, but he was going to share his good fortune and invite Dooley to live with him."

His voice remained hard. "It stands to reason, whoever came to the door was let in by Dooley."

I moved on. "Is it possible I wasn't the only one he was stalking?"

"I'm listening."

"What about the woman caller? Maybe her boyfriend or brother or dad killed Dooley because he wouldn't leave her alone."

"It's possible."

I searched for other options that didn't point to premeditation. "What if Dooley had ordered pizza and was expecting a delivery?" Even to my ears, the thought of a chef of Dooley's caliber ordering out sounded lame. And this didn't explain his worried state or the phone call that had bothered him.

"Don't think so. No sign of pizza or pizza boxes anywhere." Romero wasn't averse to hearing other ideas, but he wasn't going to give credence to notions plucked out of thin air.

That didn't stop me from coming up with another scenario. "Perhaps he'd heard a cat in the alley. Maybe he went to check on it, and he met trouble."

By the silence on the other end, Romero was either considering this or deciding *I* was cuckoo. "For a random act, someone went to a lot of trouble to snuff out Dooley."

I thought about discovering Dooley in the beer keg. "Yeah. There is that."

"Whatever the reason Dooley went to the door, someone—likely the assailant—shoved him back into the restaurant, probably had an altercation with him, knocked him unconscious, stuffed him in a barrel, and shot him point-blank."

I grimaced. "That's a lot of assumptions."

"Backed by facts. Shuffled tables. Tipped chairs. No blood anywhere except in the barrel. And bruises on the victim. I expect the coroner will confirm he was assaulted."

Repulsion clogged my throat, the picture Romero painted almost too much to bear. If I'd been able to squelch the squeamishness when we'd discovered Dooley's body, I might've noticed these things for myself.

Romero paused in a way that told me he'd disclosed enough, then said he had to go. I stared out the driver's side window, thankful I'd learned this much. Still, I couldn't wipe the grim expression off my face. "Okay. See you."

He paused again, and this time I knew it was because he didn't want to say goodbye. I didn't want to say goodbye either. My fears were growing, and safety was an issue. If I hadn't been so determined to see this thing through, I would've taken Romero up on his offer to protect me. Shoot. Why was it so hard to play it safe?

"Oh, for Pete's sake," Max cried next to me. "Will you hang up already?"

I jumped at his voice, gave him a dirty look, then disconnected the phone.

We drove to the station, and I listened to Max go on about all the pastry recipes he could try if he'd taken the bread machine. "I could've even made pizza dough." He slid me a sly look. "You know how much you love doughy pizzas."

I squealed to a stop in the bumpy police parking lot, threw the gear in park, and glared at Max. "Look, if you want the bread machine, then take it. I'm not stopping you."

"Technically, you were."

"Hey, it's not my hips the carbs will cling to."

Max drew his eyes into tiny slits. "If Mr. Long Arm of the Law knew how you were talking to me, he'd think twice before sucking on those luscious vanilla-scented lips of yours."

Oh boy.

Sexy thoughts of Romero's deft caresses and passionate kisses came to mind, kisses that revealed how hot-blooded and easily aroused he was. I wanted to turn back the clock to when we were in each other's arms. No homicides to think about. No dreadful deliveries. I merely wanted to feel that hunger again. But with another murder case on Romero's hands, who knew when I'd see him next?

I buried those thoughts and calmed my voice. "I just don't want you complaining that you've gained weight. But if you have your heart set on the bread machine, then you have my blessing."

I grabbed my bag and bundled up my coat. "I'll be a few minutes. Want to come with me?"

"I've had my fill of police stations lately, thank you very much."

Max had wound up in a Puerto Rican jail while we'd been on the cruise. He'd barely gotten over his ordeal, and I wasn't going to push the matter.

"But do me a favor," he added. "Run a brush through your hair. Between your poked eye and that lump of tangled mess on your crown, you're embarrassing me."

"Gee, sorry. I wouldn't want to make you look bad." I gave him a caustic look, then flipped down my sun visor and gawked at myself in the mirror. "What's everyone talking about? My eye isn't even red anymore."

"Your eye makeup is still smudged."

Critic.

I whipped a tissue out of my bag, dabbed it around my eye, and got rid of the smudges. Then I swept a brush through my hair. It didn't help as much as I'd hoped, but it was enough to receive only a minor eye roll from Max.

I went into the station, dropped off the photos with minimal harassment, and angled back into the car.

Max granted me a solemn look. "You're right about the bread maker."

I heaved out a sigh. "That again?"

"It's okay. I don't want the thing. I'm over it."

I started the engine. "Thank God for small mercies."

My next stop was Rivers View. There was an inmate I wished to speak to. Since I was driving by Waltham, where Max lived, I could drop him off at his condo on the way. I didn't need to listen to him pining about the bread machine for the rest of the day. And if I knew Max, he wasn't over it as he'd declared.

I hopped onto I-95, and Max looked from the road to me. "If you think you're taking me home, you've got another thing coming."

I gave him a sideways glance. "What's that supposed to mean?"

"It *means* Romero took me aside before we left the restaurant and made me promise not to let you out of my sight." He took a quick breath. "And before you say anything on the matter, I value my life more than my job. So if you're going to fire me, go right ahead."

I fumed silently, adding turncoat to Max's list of traits. "Fine. Then you won't mind coming to the pokey with me to visit Luther Boyle."

He whacked his hand on the dashboard in shock. "*Luther Boyle!* As in the Luther Boyle who killed Freddie?"

"At least one of the killers, yes. And sidekick to Ziggy Stoaks."

Max gulped. "Why are you visiting Luther Boyle?"

I filled him in on Ziggy's escape and told him I wanted to question Boyle. The men were buddies, after all. I was confident the still-imprisoned half of the duo would know something about Ziggy's breakout.

"Let me get this straight." Max tapped his fingertips on the dashboard. "A dildo was delivered to you this morning, and because Ziggy fled from jail and quite possibly could be walking on sunshine or tiptoeing through the tulips, you believe he was the postmaster."

"That's the gist of it." His reference to old tunes wasn't lost on me. When the mood suited him, Max could be a wordsmith, a player of terms, a gigolo of jive. Well, I could *parlez-vous* with the best of them. "I'd bet anything he was the one getting dirty deeds done dirt cheap."

"Touché." He nodded at my AC/DC line. "You think Luther's going to tell you anything?"

"I won't know until I get there." I gave him a sly grin, conjuring up a Supertramp oldie. "I'm hoping he'll give a little bit of his time to me."

"*Enough* already." He peered ahead at the road, likely assessing the visitation situation.

"This is your last chance," I said, hands on the wheel. "I can take the next exit to your place, and you won't have to enter another jail."

He puffed out his cheeks. The thing about Max was he could be unpredictable. At times he'd laugh in the face of danger, the risk taker, a smart-alecky Rambo. Then there were other times he'd scream like a banshee if someone said *boo*. I spied him out of the corner of my eye, looking earnest.

He finally blew out air. "Onward. And no more silly song references."

I shrugged, continuing down the highway. "Don't say I didn't warn you."

Chapter 5

I traveled south of Boston until we entered the pretty town of Norfolt. Leaves scattered from trees, and the sun beamed down on gazebos, churches, a library, and quaint-looking shops. A virtual fall-destination postcard. The library had a sign on the lawn stating the day and time of the next town hall meeting.

"I think we've arrived in Stars Hollow," Max purred.

"Stars Hollow?"

He sighed in frustration. "You know! *Gilmore Girls?* Luke's Diner? *Luke?* Who, by the way, bears a striking resemblance to that handsome cop of yours."

I smiled, remembering the show I'd watched as a teen. And laughing at Luke's grouchy disposition. Undeniably, there were similarities to Romero. "You want me to drop you off so you can find Luke and the gang?"

"Don't be funny. I loved Stars Hollow. It reminded me of Rueland."

"Rueland is a lot bigger than Stars Hollow. And Rueland—" I clamped my mouth shut. Why was I debating Max about Rueland and a fictional town? "If you like Rueland so much, why not move there? It'd be handier than driving back and forth to Waltham every day." This wasn't an issue for Max since he powered his car with rocket fuel and arrived at work in less time than it took to paint my nails.

"All in good time, lovey. All in good time."

We picked up a couple of take-out slices of pizza from a quaint restaurant, and Max yammered on about the bread machine. "This pizza's paper thin. See how the toppings stick like glue? If I had a certain bread machine—whose past owner shall remain nameless—you could have all the pizzas you like. The toppings would be so fresh they'd be begging you to take a bite. And it'd all be because of the scrumptious homemade dough."

I turned over the engine, shot him a look, and gnawed on my pizza. We drove out of the colonial area in silence, past homes, forests, and the odd farm. Five miles south of Norfolt, I exited down a quiet paved road. After a few twists and turns, we arrived at our destination.

The gate boasted a sign that said Rivers View Correctional Center. Beside the name was a logo depicting jail bars with water streaming through them. Not sure how I felt about being here, I took a brave breath and rolled past the gate into the facility's parking lot.

Rivers View was a large square building with a series of smaller buildings set behind the main structure. Hotel accommodations for the inmates, complete with barbed-wire fencing.

Max and I assessed the grounds in doubtful reserve. Neither one of us said anything, but if his thoughts were in tune with mine, we were in trouble.

"Bottoms up," he ventured at last, cheering with an invisible glass.

We paraded into the main building, where we were searched and asked to show our identification. The uniforms hadn't mentioned my past. But by the glint in their eyes, I was convinced they knew. I'd seen the same glint so many times, it was a wonder I'd never been blinded by all the sparks. After they looked in my bag, they shared another look. Then I was told to lock my belongings in my car.

Max yanked me off to the side in a huff. "What'd you bring that in here for? You know it's an arsenal of beauty weapons."

Like I was going to break an inmate out of jail with a jar of face cream. I shook my head in disgust, ignoring the surrounding monitors. *Fine.* I didn't argue the point. It was a good point, too, considering my history of catching crooks using my beauty tools.

Once we were deemed worthy to proceed, I asked if visiting hours had begun. We were in luck. It was one o'clock. Visiting hours were about to kick off. But we hadn't been pre-approved to see Luther Boyle. This posed a problem.

"Now what?" Max pushed me into the main visitors' section, hounding me like I was an oracle with all the answers.

Overlooking his expectant stare, I turned for inspiration to the chatty crowd lined up at the visitation room door.

"Get back in line, you little turd!" a woman's voice bellowed over the others.

Immediately, a hush fell over the crowd, and a tall, well-built man in a suit and tie, who I assumed was the warden, hustled over to see what the trouble was. That's when I caught a glimpse of the trouble.

I blinked twice in disbelief. But there was no mistaking it. Candace Needlemeyer. Archenemy number one. Her blond hair was twisted up in a bun, and she was shaking her fake boobs furiously in Little Turd's face.

"What's Candace doing here?" Max wanted to know.

"Maybe she's training to be a guard," I said, half joking.

"Maybe she's here to do someone's hair."

We looked at each other. Would Candace drive all the way from Supremo Stylists to Norfolt to do an inmate's hair? "Nah," we said in unison.

A small part of me still brooded over whether Candace was capable of planting a dildo on my porch. But I swept that thought aside and watched the warden usher her away from the short man and order them both to take a seat.

"That little turd thought he could sneak in front of me," she argued. "Why do *I* have to sit?"

"You've been here before," the warden said. "You should know better."

Candace had been here before? Max and I looked at each other, eyebrows stretched to our hairlines.

She tightened her lips, strutted over to a chair, and before sitting, she reared her head in our direction.

"What are you gawking at?" She pranced over in her five-inch black stilettos, peering down her nose at me in my own four-inch heels.

"Hi to you, too, Candace." I smiled sweetly. "We're visiting an inmate." Like we were going to market to buy a fat pig. "You?"

She folded her arms over her large silicone-filled breasts and tapped her toe on the tiled floor. "What do you know? We have something in common. I'm here to see an inmate, too. Family, actually."

"I thought Charles Manson died," Max said.

Candace narrowed her gaze on Max, and I could've sworn I saw flames.

I eyed her suspiciously, wondering again if she had been the culprit in this morning's delivery. "Shouldn't you be shopping for dildos to fill in for your next big date?" It was a low blow, but it took a lot to insult Candace.

She stuck her nose in the air. "I've never touched a dildo in my life."

I sighed, deflated, because I had a feeling she was telling the truth.

"I'm here to see my grandpa, Two-Notes."

"Two-Notes?" I put my previous thoughts to bed and concentrated on this name that had a familiar ring to it.

"What's your grandpa doing here?" Max asked.

"None of your beeswax." With that, she turned and huffed away.

I thought with some surprise how most people would've

held their heads low when visiting a relative in prison. Not Candace. She'd said her grandpa's name as if he were up for best actor of the year.

"Great," I said. "Here I was thinking Candace might be our *in*."

"An in for what?" a deep voice said behind us, startling both Max and me.

We whipped around and faced Jock looking all sexy and in control, like he had this morning at the restaurant after we'd discovered Dooley's body...and *before* we'd discovered Dooley's body.

"Uh..." Max stuttered.

I wasn't going to be intimidated by Jock, even if Max was close to passing out from Mr. Argentina's overpowering presence. I crossed my arms in front like Candace had, though I didn't have the huge chest to go with the fierce attitude. "An *in* to see an inmate."

"Who do you want to see?" Jock looked intrigued, but I wasn't buying it.

"Luther Boyle," I said matter-of-factly. "Know him?"

Jock grinned. "Know *of* him. In prison for murdering Max's friend." He paused, his look directed at me. "Heard he has several scars on his stomach due to wounds from the sharp end of a metal tail comb. Looks like he'd had his gallbladder removed laparoscopically."

"Ha. Ha. So I punctured a few holes in him. He's behind bars, isn't he?"

"That, he is."

"What are *you* doing here?" As if I didn't already know.

"Same thing as you, I suspect. Looking for answers. Heard Luther's friend Ziggy Stoaks escaped last night."

I raised my chin. "I take it you heard this from Romero."

His grin widened. "I swore scout's honor I wouldn't reveal where I learned it."

Perfect. "I assume you also want to talk to Luther."

"That's a fair assumption."

I looked over at the crowd. "Then why aren't you in line like the rest of the visitors?"

He glanced over his shoulder at the warden. "Darryl's giving me private access."

"The plot thickens," Max murmured.

I backhanded Max in the stomach, turning a deaf ear to his grunt. My gaze flitted from Jock, to the monitors, to the warden who was resettling in his glassed-in office, the glass, most likely, bulletproof. "This Darryl a friend of yours?"

"You could say that. He does a little stunt work on the side."

As did Jock. Not only did he have a background in the navy, but he also did stunt-doubling when he could afford the time.

"We were in a film together a few years ago. Kept in touch." He nodded toward the office where his black leather jacket hung on the back of a chair next to Darryl. "Had a good visit at lunch."

I took this all in. "Since you're on such good terms with Darryl, do you think he would let us in to question Luther Boyle?"

He crossed his arms, his muscles bulging through his long-sleeved, tightly knit shirt. "Let's break this down. You haven't been approved to visit Luther, have you?"

"Uh, no."

"And you want me to fix it so you can."

I forced myself to look him in the eye. "When you put it that way...*yes*."

"What's in it for me?"

Max gave a high whimper behind me.

"Anything you want," I said, Miss Bold amongst a crowd.

"Anything?"

A spark of danger ignited in his eyes, and immediately I took back my words. "Maybe not...*anything*."

He took a daunting step closer. His exotic citrus scent, mixed with the smell of leather that still clung to him, tested my self-control. "What about a nighttime ride on my Harley?"

I'd ridden on Jock's bike once before and had almost kissed the ground when I'd gotten off. Not that I didn't trust his driving skills, but some of us preferred a roof and four doors surrounding us when we drove.

I ordered my hormones to settle down and choked back a cough at his suggestion. "A nighttime ride? Where would we go?"

"You'll see." His voice was low, almost a whisper.

I gulped back the promise of those words, ignoring the shiver racing through my body.

A bike ride wasn't such a fuss. Probably cruise around Rueland and be home before bedtime. Thing was, I didn't have a chance at seeing Luther Boyle without Jock's help. I bit the bullet and put out my hand. "Deal."

He looked from my eyes down to my hand, gripping it warmly in his.

I almost peed my pants from the strength and sensuality of his grasp. *You're such an idiot, Valentine. Acting all tough. Now look at the predicament you're in.*

I tightened my thighs and straightened my spine, showing how fearless I could be.

"Let me see what I can do." He sauntered off to talk to Darryl.

As soon as his back was turned, Max slapped my shoulder. "Are you crazy?"

"Ow!" I rubbed my shoulder. "What do you mean?"

"You know what Jock's going to do with you when he gets you alone on that bike?"

"Nothing," I replied firmly.

"*Nothing!*" He lowered his voice. "Do you know how many riding positions there are on a motorcycle? And I don't mean positions riding the highway."

Max had gotten a lift in this morning on Jock's bike and suddenly he was King of the Hog. Still, that didn't make him sex expert Dr. Ruth.

I dragged him over to a private corner. "If I can get in to speak to Luther, I'll give Jock a few hours of my time…even if it's on his Harley."

He dropped his chin to his chest. "You better be prepared to lose your undies in the process." He grinned. "Jock's proven to be proficient at removing those."

I kept my expression neutral. Not that Max knew this, but the one time Jock got me naked, I wasn't wearing undies.

Non-contact visitation was normally limited to two people at a time, but Darryl obviously made an exception in our case.

We tramped into a long room and took a cubicle behind a glass window. There were two chairs and two phones on our side of the glass, plus a small ledge. Max sat to my right, and Jock stood behind us like a guard.

I had to admit I was relieved I wouldn't be able to reach out and touch Luther Boyle. I was doubly relieved he wouldn't be able to reach out and strangle me.

I hiccupped back my unease at that thought and looked past the two women on my left to Candace. She scraped her chair up to the glass window, wiggled her tush until she was comfortable, then slanted forward, tapping her nails impatiently on the ledge in front of her.

I didn't want to seem intrusive, so I turned back to our window and waited for the prisoners to be brought in. At the same time, I picked up the conversation between Max and Jock behind me.

"Bank robbery!" Max's eyes almost popped out of his head.

Jock stood arms crossed, nodding. "Back in the fifties, I believe."

I frowned, piecing together their exchange. "What was back in the fifties?"

Jock tilted his head toward Candace. "Her grandfather Two-Notes was one of the most notorious bank robbers on the East Coast. During a robbery, he'd wear a green eye mask with dollar signs on it. Steal everything he could get his hands on. Supposedly once even yanked out a teller's gold tooth. His calling card was leaving two one-dollar bills behind as a tip for doing business. Hence the name Two-Notes."

Max and I gaped openly in Candace's direction. I recalled hearing something about a gangster named Two-Notes years and years ago, long before I'd met Candace. It was spine-chilling yet fascinating.

Jock rested his hands on the back of my chair, recapturing our attention. "It was decades before he was finally caught and sentenced to life in prison. I presume family life suffered."

Holy smokes. What a story. What had Candace's grandfather been like? What impact had he had on Candace, only seeing her through a glass window? I peered back at Max. He swallowed solemnly, probably wondering the same thing.

We heard a heavy door automatically slide open from the far left on the other side of the glass, and one by one the inmates trudged in wearing yellow jumpsuits. Luther Boyle was the first inmate to enter the room. At once, fear swelled inside me, and I couldn't find my breath.

I told myself to pull it together. Lots of people paid visits here daily, and nothing violent happened to them. Plus, two guards and a woman in a white lab coat stood in the background, keeping their eyes peeled for any suspicious behavior. I didn't know what they expected could happen during a non-contact visit, but I felt safer all the same knowing prisoners were behind a glass wall.

Luther shuffled over to our cubicle, and I steeled myself inside and out. I wasn't about to hide behind Max or Jock. I'd decided to come here, and I was going to find answers to my questions.

In the years since Luther had been in prison, he'd gained more weight and lost more hair. He'd already been bald and pudgy, but his baldness had spread, and now even his eyebrows were sparse. Maybe Phyllis could practice her new skills on him.

Luther slumped in the chair opposite Max and me and gave me a venomous look. I couldn't blame him. If I'd been in his shoes, I wouldn't have been too happy to see me either.

Max poked me in the ribs, indicating I should say something.

I gave a little finger wave through the glass, more nervous than I thought I'd be.

Jock leaned in. "It helps if you pick up the phone."

I clenched my hands open and shut. "Right."

Max and I selected our phones, and Luther grabbed his. I got right to it, asking what he knew about Ziggy's escape.

He looked at me as if he wondered if I was for real. "Lady, I got scars on my belly and suffer nightmares in my cell because of you. You think I'm going to tell you anything about Zig's escape?"

I shrugged. "Yes?"

He smushed his face to the glass and kissed it. In other words, forget it.

Behind Luther's shoulder, the woman in the white lab coat said something to him. He angled back in his chair, phone close to his ear. "Even if I did know something, these walls have ears. Hell, the floors have ears. And I don't care to make my life here any worse than it is."

Jock plucked the phone from Max and gave a laser-sharp stare through the glass at Luther. "When was the last time you spoke to Stoaks?"

Luther looked up at Jock like he'd come face to face with his nemesis Superman. For a second, he was speechless. "I don't remember. Few days ago. Maybe a week."

"Did he ever mention Valentine's name, say he was going to get even?"

I peeked up at Jock taking control, and my heart gave a brazen thump. Swallowing in admiration, I stared back at Luther, witnessing the begrudging respect in his eyes as well.

"Sure, he'd joke about it occasionally. Lots of inmates mutter the same thing. 'Gonna get even with the scum who put me behind bars.' But I never believed it for a minute. All talk as far as I could see."

Jock handed the phone back to Max, and Luther shifted in his seat, letting out a breath.

"What's this all about anyway?" Luther refocused on me. "Why all the questions about Zig?"

I switched the phone to my other ear, then laid it out for Luther. "I got a delivery on my doorstep this morning, and I think Ziggy may have been responsible for it."

"What kind of delivery?" He edged forward, genuinely interested.

I lowered my voice into the phone. "A perm rod wrapped around a dildo."

"Ha-ha-ha!" he barked in a fit of laughter, slapping his pudgy hand on his knee. "What goes around comes around."

He wiped the tears from his eyes, straightening in his chair. "Listen, Zig and I might have committed murder and run a puppy mill, but we weren't all that close. If you want to know the truth, I don't know what happened to him. So if that's all, take a hike." He gave me a last once-over. "And buy a brush, why don't you. You're a disgrace to the profession." Then he hung up.

I scowled at his rudeness and self-consciously ran a finger through my hair for the umpteenth time today. Many more of these insults, and I was going to shave my head bald like Luther.

Max reached for my phone, then propped both receivers back in their cradles. "That went well."

We were watching Luther disappear through the door he'd entered through when Candace hijacked our attention, pounding the glass in front of her. "Grandpa! Wake up!"

We craned our necks to see Candace's grandpa on the other side of the window. I blinked twice in surprise.

Two-Notes wasn't one of those tall legendary bank robbers like Warren Beatty from *Bonnie and Clyde*, with a charming smile and a glorious head of hair. He was more of a I-need-my-walker-and-false-teeth bank robber who was probably past his naptime.

My mouth hung open in shock. I couldn't see Two-Notes holding up a comb, let alone a bank.

"That's Two-Notes?" Max's jaw hung lower than mine.

"That's him," Jock said.

"He's bald…and stooped over." Max slanted to get a better look. "And he's drooling."

"He's not a young man anymore," Jock replied.

While Max was getting over his crushed fantasy of what Candace's grandfather would look like, Jock nodded at me. "You didn't think you'd learn any more from Boyle, did you?"

I scraped back my chair and stood. "I didn't know what I thought, but coming here felt like the right thing to do." I crossed my arms and gazed up into his caramel-flecked eyes. "Do you think Ziggy planted that dildo on my porch?" No sense pretending Jock hadn't heard. He always knew more than he let on.

My dead stalker was another option. But I preferred not to share this with Jock or the fact that Dooley had been stalking me. It was better to let Romero handle this since the two men were already too cozy as far as I was concerned.

"I'm not sure. But we're going to find out."

"We?"

He raised a sexy eyebrow. "You don't like the sound of that?"

I liked it more than he knew. But I was starting to feel smothered by all the sudden attention. "Let me guess. Romero told you to keep an eye on me."

"He's a wise man." A grin slid up his face. "And I'm only too happy to oblige."

Chapter 6

"**D**o you two want to get a room?" Max asked.

Jock lost the grin and stared deep into my eyes. "I don't know." He paused. "Do we?"

A nervous giggle escaped me, and I clapped a hand over my mouth. The thought of consummating our relationship almost gave me heart failure. That's not to say I hadn't considered it. I had. I just didn't know how wise it'd be to sleep with an employee who was Hercules in the flesh, who had women falling at his feet, who made my heartbeat race.

Then there was Romero. Gorgeous. Stubborn. Macho. Cop.

All right. So I had two hot men in my life who triggered erotic thoughts…thoughts I'd never experienced before. I had determination. I could keep those thoughts bottled away.

"Don't be funny." I stiffened at Max.

"Who's joking?" he retorted.

I pushed past both of them and exited the building. Things were getting complicated, and I needed a moment to think clearly.

Max was on my heels, babbling about me losing my undies, and I whipped around like a shot.

"Look. My day started with me poking and burning my

eye with a mascara wand, then progressed to worse when my hair wouldn't cooperate." I raked a finger through my hairline, silently blaspheming it. "*Then*, it got even more interesting when I discovered a fat dildo on my porch. If *that* wasn't an indicator that I should've gone back to bed, discovering Jimmy's dead cousin *was*."

Max opened his mouth to speak but snapped it shut when I swung my palm an inch from his face.

"*Now*," I continued, "we have an escaped psychopath who's scaring me senseless, photos that show Dooley was stalking me, plus, there's a murderer who may have had it in for Dooley or who may be a serial killer. Only time will tell. On top of all this, questioning Luther Boyle about Ziggy proved futile."

I stamped to Daisy Bug, unlocked the doors, and smacked my hand on the roof. "And to round things off, Jock's planning something devious which may or may not involve the removal of undies, you've got an obsession with a bread maker, and Romero's apparently got a pack of bloodhounds trailing me."

Max sniffed, his nose out of joint. "I'd rather not be referred to as a bloodhound...if you don't mind."

Oh brother. "Where'd Jock go anyway?"

Max looked over his shoulder. "I don't know. I think he went to talk to Darryl."

"Wonderful. Well, I'm not hanging around here another minute."

Max scooted to the other side of the car and hopped inside like I was Batman and he was Robin. "Where are we going next?"

I angled into the car and slid the key in the ignition. "I'm not sure. But something Luther said back there got me thinking."

"About what?"

I fixed my gaze on the dashboard, going over the recent conversation, but I couldn't retrieve what he'd said that struck a chord. "It'll come to me."

"I can tell you *this*." Max faced me. "If Luther was

telling the truth, and he really *doesn't* know where Ziggy is, you'd better have eyes in the back of your head, because, that dildo, sugar? That was a direct calling card."

His voice was stern. "And if you don't like the bloodhounds Romero assigned to you, then you'd better start looking for killer German shepherds to guard you because you're going to need protection." He spun forward, jerked his seatbelt across his toned abs, and clicked it loudly into place.

Drama queen. I started the engine, thinking of a way I could dump Max, when my cell phone chimed in my bag, shattering what was left of my fragile nerves.

I dragged it out and sighed at the readout. My mother.

"Aren't you going to answer it?" Max said.

I blinked miserably at him and answered the phone.

Just my luck. I'd forgotten that this afternoon I was supposed to pick up Tantig, my father's aunt. She had recently moved in with my parents, and I'd agreed to take her to Kuruc's European Deli.

My parents lived in Burlington, and Kuruc's was in Rueland, down and across the street from my shop. A short drive from one town to the other, but not something I wished to do at the moment.

I tapped my fingers on the steering wheel, thinking about my obligations. Darn. Not only had I forgotten about Tantig, but I'd sworn I was going to drop off the new stack of magazines at the salon that were piling up in my trunk and that I kept forgetting about when I went to work. Why did everything have to happen at once? Well, I wasn't going to make a bunch of trips. *And* I needed to get Max off my back.

Hold on. The shop was a short drive from Jimmy's, where a certain bread machine was calling Max's name. And Jimmy's was on a route I could take to my parents'. Hmm. Drop off the magazines. Lose Max. Pick up Tantig.

I hadn't solved a Rubik's Cube, and I'd probably never understand the stock market, but this felt pretty damn good.

I told my mother I'd be there in an hour, then hung up with a smart plan in place. "How'd you like to get that bread maker?" I smiled shrewdly at Max.

He cut me a sidelong glance. "What do you have going on in that sweet head of yours?"

Even when Max suspected me of double-dealing, he remained complimentary. "Nothing immoral. I promised my mother I'd take Tantig to Kuruc's. She's making Armenian *sarma* today and needs more grape leaves."

He sliced me a suspicious look. "Why can't your mother take her?"

"Because she's up to her elbows baking for the Christmas bazaar. And before you ask about my father, he's in a bowling tournament today."

He pursed his lips like he was considering whether to believe all this. "I fail to see where I come in with the bread maker."

I revved the engine, offering him a coaxing grin. "I need to drop off some magazines at the shop, and then we'll be passing right by Jimmy's. You know you're dying to try that machine."

He tilted his head in agreement and stared straight ahead. "Okay. To Jimmy's."

I smiled so wide that my idea was working I probably resembled the village idiot. I reined in my enthusiasm, gave a firm nod, and before Max figured out my ruse, I zoomed out of the parking lot.

"This isn't the way to Jimmy's," Max commented twenty minutes later. We cruised down Darling, nearing the shop. "And there's Kuruc's. Why not pick up the grape leaves now?"

We passed the bank and Rueland Travel on our right. The drugstore, Dilly's Florist, and Kuruc's—where I'd be returning to later—were on our left.

"It's a shortcut. I want to drop off the magazines first, remember?" How could he remember when his head was filled with thoughts of pizza dough and pastry?

I eased up on the gas pedal. "And grape leaves aren't the only item Tantig will want when we go to Kuruc's. Last time I took her there, I had five bags of groceries to lug out to the car."

I was about to turn into the parking lot I shared with Friar Tuck's when Max clutched my arm and screamed.

"What the *heck*!" I slammed on the brakes, almost veering into the donut shop's huge glass window.

"Look!" He pointed a shaky arm at my salon next door.

Drawn on the front window under the striped awning and swirly sign that read BEAUMONT'S was a large penis with a perm rod clipped around the base. The words *I'M BAA-ACK* were scribbled across it.

I moved to the edge of my seat and blinked twice. How much more were things going to escalate? The dildo delivery this morning was bad enough. If there was any doubt earlier, this seemed to point straight at Stoaks.

Determined to remain calm, I took a cautious glance out my driver's-side window. "Good thing it's Sunday and traffic is slow. Maybe nobody's seen it."

Three cars whizzed by, and one driver blared the horn.

"Nobody's *seen* it!" Max gaped back at the shop. "Look at it! It's bold and black and standing as erect as the Bunker Hill Monument."

The drawing was nowhere near the size of the tower built to commemorate the historic Revolutionary War battle, but tell Max that.

I swerved into the parking lot past Friar Tuck's mini stone castle and screeched to a stop behind the buildings. I clasped my bag and we raced inside the shop, flicking on the lights on the way to the dispensary—our supply room and hangout between clients. Max ran soapy water into a bucket. I called the police on the French provincial phone that sat on the counter across from the sink.

"Don't clean the window yet." I set the fancy handset

back on its cradle. "The police will want to see it." Like I was looking forward to that.

Within minutes, two uniforms arrived with another ID unit. Romero was nowhere in sight. I was looking up in silent prayer about that when my cell phone jingled.

I retrieved my bag from the counter in the dispensary and hauled out my phone, not too thrilled that the readout said it was Romero.

"Heard you had some excitement at the salon."

Boy, news traveled fast. "You could say that."

"Max with you?"

Max was outside with the cops, making grand sweeping gestures at the front window. I tightened my grip on the phone, irked that Romero had assigned Max to stick by my side. "Yes." But not for long, I thought smugly.

"Good. Stoaks is having his fun, but he'll slip up. Don't worry. We'll catch him."

Easy for *him* to say. He wasn't the one being chased by a fake penis.

"Before we go on," he said, "thought you might like to know the time of Dooley's death puts it at roughly 10:45 p.m. Also, Jimmy's alibi is rock-solid. He didn't leave the poker game until after one in the morning."

I gave an inward huff. I didn't need to be told Jimmy was innocent. "Terrific."

I watched a cop take photos and dust the glass outside. "Any news on the real apparatus? Fingerprints? Date or store where it was purchased?"

"Nothing." He gave a tired exhale. "Checked every adult-merchandise shop from Norfolt to Rueland. Sex toys are extremely popular, and dildos are bought as often as bubblegum. Every size and color under the rainbow."

"What? Who cares about style preferences? We simply need to know if a guy with a limp purchased one sometime in the hours before it was placed on my porch."

"First of all..." Romero cleared his throat. "The limp is no longer."

"What do you mean?"

"The file on Stoaks states he had a large gash on his calf at the time of the perm-rod incident. Seems one of his puppy-mill pups had taken a chunk out of his leg, causing a temporary limp. But the undeserving bastard healed."

Lucky for him. If he hadn't been sitting by his lawyer the whole time during the trial, I might have noticed this for myself.

"And if I had the manpower," Romero continued, "I'd search every store in the state of Massachusetts. But the truth is, Stoaks wouldn't have used a credit card unless he'd stolen it, and without some type of tracking, a search is almost impossible. However, if we could locate the correct store, and he'd lifted the dildo but used a stolen credit card on other purchases, we might be able to track him. But again, that would take a lot more manpower than I have."

"Great."

"Doesn't make me happy either. Stoaks is our most likely suspect *and* a convicted murderer on the run. When it comes down to it, the details of the acquired dildo are immaterial. We're going to catch the snake whether he delivered the item to your door or not."

"Good to hear." I paced back and forth behind the four ivory-colored styling chairs in the salon, the grapevines and twinkling lights that wove across the four wood-framed mirrors on the wall catching my eye. "Where does that leave us?"

"Us?"

Oops. I'd forgotten Romero thought I'd done my duty today, holding Jimmy's hand and dropping off the photos at the police station. Of course, I wasn't sure what his bloodhounds had reported. But all things considered, I wasn't going to ask. "I mean you…and Rueland's wonderful police department."

"I know what you mean. And I think we've been down this road before." I could've sworn I heard him growl. "Before I completely lose my cool, you want to tell me why you went to Rivers View to visit Luther Boyle?"

Aha. I opened my mouth to respond, but his voice increased another decibel. "Bad enough you're in the middle of this whole damn murder mess. You had no business going to a correctional facility to question an inmate about Stoaks."

The hairs on the back of my neck pricked up at his tone. "And *you* had no business leashing Max and Jock to my side until death do us part."

I was glad I couldn't see Romero. I had a feeling his strong hands were clenching, his unshaved jaw tensing.

"If you're not careful," he ground out, "death will come sooner than you think."

I wasn't sure if he meant by the hands of a killer like Ziggy or by the hands of a particular detective. Either way, I wasn't going to stand here and listen to any more threats.

I snatched a hairbrush from my station's drawer and rapped it lightly on the side of my phone, causing a bristly, scratching sound. "What? Can't hear you. You're breaking up…"

"Valentine—"

I disconnected with a self-satisfied click, tossed the brush in the drawer, and dropped my phone in my bag.

After the cops finished their business, I dug out some rags, and Max and I cleaned the front window. Just as we were splashing it with fresh water, the pimply-faced kid who worked at Friar Tuck's sauntered outside in his medieval tunic and felt crown.

"Gee," he croaked. "What'd you do that for?"

"Excuse me?" I wiped away a bead of water running down the front of my jacket.

"Why'd you wash off the cool artwork? It's the talk of the town."

"Grand." I picked up the wet rags from the ground. "Did you happen to see who painted the cool artwork?"

He shrugged. "Nope. Too busy serving coffee and donuts."

"What about anyone else?" I gestured to the bakery. "Someone must've seen something."

"Nope. Cops came by, asked the same questions. All I saw were pictures on everyone's phones. None showed Michelangelo at work." He hunched forward and traipsed back into Friar Tuck's.

Max rolled his eyes. "I'm surprised that kid can roll a donut in sugar." He straightened. "Hey, that's something else I can make with the bread machine. Donuts!"

I dumped the rags in the bucket. "Right. Jimmy's awaits."

And I could leave behind a bloodhound.

Chapter 7

We swung into Jimmy's driveway several minutes later and found him exiting the garage with a book in hand. He put on a faint smile and gave us one of his surfer-dude waves, but I could tell his heart wasn't into it.

My insides mellowed for the Skink. Everything had seemed to be going right in his life. A new home. New business. New outlook. And now sorrow had struck.

Instead of dropping off Max like I'd planned, I parked and ambled up the driveway with him. I knew time was ticking, and Tantig would be waiting, but being late was better than calling and confessing what had happened today.

"How's it going?" I asked Jimmy.

"Hey, dudette. Max. Like, I've had better days." He hiked his thumb over his shoulder. "Detective Romero was here earlier and—"

"He was?" I stopped in my tracks. "When, earlier?"

He gave a small shrug. "Few hours ago. Like, after you left here, and before now. Wanted more info on the photos you found."

Of course. Why wouldn't Romero have followed up on my discovery? He was a detective, wasn't he? "What did you tell him?"

"Not much I *could* tell him that he didn't already know." He raised his bushy black eyebrows until they disappeared behind his springy blond curls. "Like, I showed him the room I showed you. He went through the boxes and confiscated Dooley's camera."

"Did he find anything else?"

Jimmy shook his head sadly. "I wished he had, dudette. I want to know who killed my cuz."

"We'll find the killer, Jimmy. Don't you worry." Never mind I was queasy inside about finding the murderer for myself. To be frank, Dooley wasn't just any dead victim. He was Jimmy's beloved cousin. And I was torn between feeling sympathetic for Jimmy's loss and being angry and afraid because Dooley had been stalking me. In general, I didn't put stalkers high on my list of friends.

Admittedly, I'd also been panicky since I'd discovered the photos. I wasn't sure where my emotions sat regarding Dooley, but one thing was certain. The sooner we found his killer, the sooner I'd learn answers and, hopefully, find peace for everyone involved.

I patted Jimmy's arm, noticing the book he was holding was a bread and pastry cookbook. I motioned to the spiral-bound hardcover. "Where'd you get this?"

"Oh, yeah." He held up the book, nodding at Max. "Here's the book you asked for."

My eyebrows went up sharply at Max.

"What!" He glared at me. "I told Jimmy I was coming back for the bread machine and asked if he had any cookbooks to go with it."

"When did you do that?"

"After we cleaned the shop window, while you were talking to one of Robin Hood's Merry Men."

Naturally. Max didn't miss a thing.

"It's okay, dudette," Jimmy said. "After Romero left, I remembered I'd taken a bunch of Dooley's cookbooks to the garage. He was bringing over box after box, and I told him I didn't want Aunt Neila's house to turn into a junkyard."

A tear slipped down Jimmy's cheek. Not only had he recently lost dear Aunt Neila, but now, Dooley. "Dools didn't like that much." He swiped away the tear surreptitiously. "I think he felt I was calling his stuff junk." He sniffed. "I wasn't, man. Truly."

Max wrapped his arm around Jimmy's shoulder. "Come on. Let's go inside and talk bread."

Max. Always one to console. And always one step ahead.

"You two go on. I need to do a short errand."

"No probs," Jimmy said. "But if you like, you can look at Dooley's stuff." He gestured to the garage. "Like, *mi casa es su casa*."

I considered this. It *would* only be a short detour. And by now, I was late anyway. I'd already gone through the boxes in the bedroom and found nothing that explained Dooley's murder or the photos of me and how the murder might be connected. I didn't know what I'd find in the garage, but if something was valuable to Dooley, like the pictures, I wanted to see it for myself.

I agreed to take a quick look and darted inside while Jimmy led Max into the house.

Jimmy had already put his personal stamp inside the garage. His beat-up pickup truck dripped oil on the cement floor, a workbench was piled with Red Sox and Celtics bobbleheads from his scalper days, and old tickets and posters of the Boston Bruins were taped to the wall. To one side a ladder and several surfboards added to the menagerie, along with a shelf of tools and another shelf dedicated to old DVDs.

In the far corner sat a stack of boxes with cookbooks sticking out. I wandered over to the boxes, knelt in front of them, and rummaged through the books in a methodical manner. I set Japanese cookbooks in one pile and diabetic cookbooks in another. Irish, Italian, African, and every other regional cuisine joined the first pile. Soups, salads, main courses, and desserts each got their own stack.

Dooley had quite a collection of cookbooks, and twenty minutes later, I'd rifled through most of them. Besides the odd dog-eared page and photocopied recipe, I couldn't find a thing pertaining to Dooley or his personal life. No notes. No more pictures of me, or anyone else for that matter. Not one clue as to why he was killed or was stalking me.

I hauled out the last book. *COOKING FOR DUMMIES*.

I flipped through the first few chapters and found simple recipes for grilled cheese sandwiches and piggies in a blanket. No wonder it was at the bottom of the box. If Dooley was as good a chef as Jimmy professed, grilled cheese sandwiches weren't something he was laboring over learning to make.

I gave up on finding anything significant and went to set the book back in the box when a small red notebook slid out. I picked up the booklet and skimmed through the pages.

I didn't browse far when I spotted my name. And Romero's. I knew Dooley had been photographing me, but now it seemed he'd also been taking notes on his thoughts and what he'd seen.

Dooley had been out of jail a couple of months now. According to these dates and entries, he'd been following me almost from the start of his release.

Valentine and Detective Romero cuddling outside retirement home, read one entry. Another said *Valentine on cell phone, talking dreamy-eyed to someone. Probably Romero again.* The more pages I flipped, the more frequent Dooley's observations.

A tremor shot down my spine. How close had he been to me? I mean, to hear me talk on my cell phone? I trembled again, somehow feeling compromised.

I kept reading and found a passage that made me sit up. *Valentine's not who I thought she was. She's not Ziggy's girlfriend. And I'm not following her anymore. If Stoaks wants her dead, he'll have to find someone else to do it.*

I gasped in shock at the words. Girlfriend? Ziggy wanted Dooley to kill me? The journal tumbled from my fingers. Sending the gross dildo messages was bad enough. But setting up my murder?

I swallowed hoarsely, mulling over this latest information.

Was it true? The two men knew each other? They must've been locked up together at Rivers View. Romero hadn't mentioned that when he'd said Dooley had been released several months ago. And since Jimmy had said Dooley once lived in New York, I'd assumed he'd been in the slammer there.

Ziggy must've lied to Dooley about me being his girlfriend so he could then use that lie to his advantage. He simply had to convince Dooley to kill me if he caught me cheating on him. Of course, that was assuming I'd been dating anyone. Could he have heard about Romero and me from prison before Dooley had been released?

Darn Romero. He was already two steps ahead of me. And what about Luther Boyle? Did he know about Dooley and this scheme? Granted, my knowledge of prisons had come mostly from the movies, but didn't inmates hang out together in the jail yard or courtyard or whatever they called it? Wasn't that where they formed relationships? Maybe not. Maybe at this prison, they didn't mix auto thieves with murderers. Either way, Luther *had* said he and Ziggy weren't all that close, so if he was telling the truth, it was possible he didn't know about this plot.

I guess I'd never learn if Luther knew Dooley since Luther had made it clear he was done sharing. That was A-Okay with me. I had no intention of going back there again. I could form my own theories without the help of an uncooperative jailbird.

The best theory was the simplest. Ziggy had known Dooley in prison where he then formed a plan when he knew Dooley was getting out and heading back to Rueland. And the plan was to ask him to hunt me down. His *girlfriend*. Keep tabs on me. And kill me if Dooley caught me cheating on him. Did Ziggy murder Dooley because Dooley wouldn't harm me?

I played this out in my mind. Suppose Ziggy escaped from prison and headed straight for Dooley's. Dooley must've been alerted or aware that his jail mate was planning an escape. Maybe Ziggy told him that himself. Or maybe Dooley had heard it on the news. Just because I didn't tune into the nightly broadcasts didn't mean the rest of the world didn't know what was happening. Perhaps a search had already been underway.

I looked down at the cookbooks and the journal. Dooley wanted his stuff safe, including this journal about me. He wanted it away from his apartment in case rats got to it. Enter the rat. Ziggy Stoaks. If Dooley knew that Ziggy had escaped, and he also knew that he wasn't going to hurt a hair on my head, that explained why he was hiding his stuff at Jimmy's. He didn't want Ziggy to find the pictures or his notes that showed he was washing his hands of this crazy plan.

Romero had said there were business cards at Dooley's place from the Wee Irish Dude. What if Ziggy had broken into the apartment, and when he didn't find Dooley there, he tracked him down at the restaurant and killed him?

Let's say Romero was right, and Dooley had opened the door for his assailant. Did Ziggy confront him about no longer stalking me? Did Dooley threaten to go to the cops? An altercation could've ensued, like Romero had said. Ziggy could've killed Dooley because the ex-con wouldn't snuff me out. Poor Dools. He'd been in prison for auto theft. He didn't deserve this.

A swarm of emotions welled up inside me from all the speculation. Not only was Jimmy making a real go of the restaurant business, but Dooley also seemed to want a clean start. I might have been deluding myself into thinking he'd died for me, but in a way, he had. He'd rejected Ziggy's request to kill me. The proof was in the journal.

The only thing that didn't add up was the woman caller at the restaurant who'd left Dooley distressed. Who was this person? And what was her connection to Dooley? The more I thought about all this, the worse I felt.

I put everything back in its place, picked up the booklet, and shoved it in my purse. Perspiration dotted my forehead, and my insides ached from the guilt eating me over Dooley's death. Not to mention the fear plaguing me over Ziggy's mission to end my life.

Despite the inner turmoil and mounting dread, I had to move forward. I wasn't going to let Ziggy Stoaks get away with murder. He needed to be stopped soon, before anyone else got hurt. And as far as I could see, I was the next person on Ziggy's list to get hurt.

I swept the back of my hand across my damp forehead and made a solemn promise to myself. If I didn't accomplish anything else in the next twenty-four hours, I'd get the man who killed Jimmy's cousin and who wanted me dead.

Chapter 8

Before I left Jimmy's, I snuck back in the house and found him and Max baking bread. Max was dusted in flour, and the countertop was a mess. This setup was ideal. Jimmy had something else to focus on, and Max was even happier than if he'd had Phyllis around to insult. Plus, I'd had enough of Max's hovering for one day.

It wasn't like I was Wonder Woman with her cool gold headband and boots, ready to take on the world alone. To tell the truth, I couldn't get past the jitters after guessing Ziggy's deadly plan. But I had to be brave. I had to put an end to this madness where this whacko was concerned. And though I loved Max, he was no Robin. Then again, I was no Batman either. But he was better off where he was...baking. The last thing I needed was a quasi crusader hindering my footsteps. I gave a decisive nod at my bold course of action and carried on.

By the time I got to my parents', it was late afternoon. Not exactly an hour later as I'd promised. And if I hadn't been so busy rummaging through cookbooks for clues instead of being the dutiful daughter, I would've given my mother a call to say I'd be late. As for the artwork on the salon window—another reason why I was delayed—I'd keep that bulletin to myself.

Before I went in to face the music, I shut off the engine,

tossed my keys in my bag, and pulled out my phone. I wasn't sure how Max would feel about being abandoned, but it wasn't fair to ditch him without an explanation.

"You'd better get right back here, missy!" Seems he wasn't too thrilled with being deserted.

"You were busy getting that bread machine up and running." I grabbed my bag, took a cursory glance over my shoulder, ruling out that I was being paranoid, and trekked into the garage. "And I'm not going to be alone. I'll have Tantig with me. We're going to Kuruc's and coming right back here. So stop worrying. I'll call you later, okay? If you need a ride home, I'll come back for you."

"Promise?"

I warmed at his devotion to me and did a three-finger salute, not that he could see it. "Scout's honor."

"You weren't a scout," he grumbled. "You weren't even a Brownie."

Boy. Appreciative or what. I hung up and click-clacked to the door, hoping my mother wouldn't be too upset by my tardiness.

My parents live in a long, ranch-style house with lots of bathrooms and no shortage of bedrooms. I'd grown up in a much smaller home in a busier neighborhood. When I moved out, they bought a house with more land and fewer neighbors because two people with no secrets needed lots of privacy. This place had never been "home" to me since I'd never lived here, but in a sense, wherever my parents lived would always be home.

I stepped into the house, the usual smell of cleaning agents replaced by the aroma of cinnamon, vanilla, and cloves. Fortunately, my mother and Tantig had been so busy baking, my presence wasn't missed. But what about the grape leaves? My mother had specifically called about the trip for these earlier.

She looked up at me, spatula in hand, apron around her waist. "What happened to your hair?"

I dropped my bag by the door and scrutinized myself in the hallway mirror. Cripes. I flattened my crown again and twisted my hair back off my shoulders. "Nothing."

"*Nothing.*" She wiped her free hand on her apron. "Looks like you got electrocuted."

"Fine. I got electrocuted."

"Don't be smart." She handed Tantig the spatula and walked over to me, focusing on my face. "Why is your eye makeup smudged? I've never seen you with smudged makeup."

"Mom! I didn't come by for an inspection. I'm here to pick up Tantig."

She turned her head to the kitchen clock and back at me. "You're a bit late."

"Yeah. Sorry about that." Not wanting to open the floor for discussion on the reasons *why* I was late, I marched to the closet, grabbed Tantig's coat, and folded it over a kitchen chair. Then I slipped a kiss on her cheek and said we could go now.

Tantig was in one of her usual polyester printed dresses, her hands were caked with dough, and her white hair was rumpled. I could fix Tantig's hair so she looked like a movie star, and the next day it'd be sticking out in every direction like Einstein's.

I took the spatula from Tantig and handed it back to my mother. Then I led Tantig over to the kitchen sink to wash her hands, keeping the conversation with my mother light. "We shouldn't be more than an hour," I said with as much conviction as I could muster, considering my mother was glaring at me over my shoulder.

"Don't pretend that nothing happened today." She crossed her arms, spatula standing straight up in her hand like a machete.

"What are you talking about?" I feigned a childlike innocence.

"The murder at Jimmy's restaurant."

Sheesh. "How did you hear about that?"

"Half the town knows." She tapped her foot for emphasis. "Even Holly knows, and she's at some drug enforcement conference in Washington this week."

Holly is my older sister who also happens to be a police detective. She came out of the womb on Christmas Day three years before I appeared on Valentine's Day. My parents thought they were being original when they picked our names. But for babies born on special occasions, it could've been worse. Holly could've been named Snowy or Frosty or Donner or Blitzen. And I could've been honored with a host of romantic terms, the most notable, Cupid. This did, however, have a cute ring to it.

Knowing Holly was away did pose a problem since I could often rely on her help when certain nameless detectives kept me at bay.

My mother gave one of her loud *ahems*, bringing me out of my daze. "Romero also called, looking for you. I told him you weren't here."

Thank heavens for that. Speaking of nameless detectives, I wasn't completely trying to avoid Romero, but he wouldn't be too happy with me after I'd hung up on him. I was hoping absence would make the heart grow fonder, but I was only fooling myself. I had new information for him, too, about the journal. I'd deliver that when I was sure he wouldn't kill me first...before Stoaks had a chance to.

Putting that thought to rest, I gazed at my mother. Her soft brown hair was pinned back, a daring streak of flour stuck to a sliver of gray. I smiled inside, remembering about a month ago when she'd had her hair done in the shop and Jimmy had wandered in. Jimmy thought my mother was *riiiiighteous* because she always had a plate of cookies ready if he ever materialized when she was there.

"So?" She gestured with the spatula. "How'd he look?"

"How'd who look?"

She whacked the spatula on the counter with impatience. "Jimmy's cousin."

"He looked dead. How do you think he looked?"

"I don't know. When you find these bodies, there's always a story behind it. You never find normal dead people. They're either tangled in cords, covered in food, or frozen like a Popsicle."

I didn't know what normal dead people looked like, but I wasn't about to tell her Dooley had been stuffed in a barrel and shot in the head. Some things were better left unsaid.

Ditto on this morning's dildo-and-perm-rod delivery. If my mother suspected I was the victim of foul play, I'd never hear the end of it. Bad enough I was coming to grips with this myself, I didn't need well-intentioned fretting from loved ones to keep me company. I'd already escaped further interference from Max—and Romero—on that score. Jock, too. Of course, there was my future ride on his Harley to worry about.

"You live your life like Rhoda Morgenstern." My mother raised her palm to the ceiling. "Carefree yet daring."

"Who?" I gaped at her like I was supposed to understand her sudden one-eighty.

"Mary's best friend from 'The Mary Tyler Moore Show.'" She gestured like I should've known who she was talking about. "Scarves on your head. Scarves on your windows. Beanbag chairs. Jeweled lamps."

I held up a finger. "I only have one beanbag chair."

Her face went deadpan. "Your life is like a TV show. The only thing missing is a husband. Someone who'll keep you from getting into these messes."

I'd seen enough TV reruns to argue the point. "From what I remember, Rhoda did get married…and she still got into trouble."

She eyed me grimly. "I don't recall Rhoda ever finding dead bodies in a restaurant."

"Maybe she didn't eat out."

The sharp silence told me she wasn't pleased with my humor. "The Wee Irish Goat was one of our favorites, too." She looked over at my great-aunt. "Wasn't it, Tantig?"

Tantig stood like a statue, watching my mother and me go at it. "They did not have *kay*-bob on the menu." She rolled her eyes in disgust at this culinary oversight.

My mother gave a patient sigh. "Shish kebab is an Armenian dish. They didn't have it on the menu because the restaurant was Irish-Italian."

"They should've had *kay*-bob." That said it all for Tantig. She wasn't impressed by Irish, Italian...or Chinese cuisine. She'd immigrated to the U.S. as a young woman during hard times, and her heart and tastes still belonged in the old country.

"The restaurant has a new owner and a new name. The Wee Irish Dude." My mother helped Tantig on with her coat. "And there's been a murder there."

"Who-hk cares?" She made the scraping noise in her throat that always trailed the word *who*.

Tantig wasn't one to mince words. It wasn't that she was heartless in the face of another murder. Her interests just didn't stretch beyond the weather channel or soap operas. If she never saw Jimmy's new restaurant or never learned more about the slaying, she wouldn't lose any sleep over it. With that, she turned her back on us, picked her patent leather purse off the floor, and trundled out the door.

Chapter 9

We'd been on the road five minutes, heading for Rueland, when we were pulled over.

I watched out my side mirror as a uniform hoisted himself from his car, slid on his peaked cap, and adjusted his gun belt like it was a Miss America ribbon. Drat. Officer Martoli, one of Rueland's famous wiseass cops.

I reached into the backseat for my own cap that I keep for bad hair days—*ha*—and plunked it on my head, hoping he wouldn't recognize me.

Martoli hauled out a notebook, strode toward my Bug, and rapped on the window.

I lowered the window, raising my voice. "Yes, officer?"

"You realize your passenger isn't wearing a seatbelt?"

I glanced at Tantig. "Uh, yeah. Sorry." After I'd had a mishap with the car a few months ago, the seatbelt warning worked when it felt like it. One thing that never quite got fixed.

"It's against the—" He stopped short, bent to look at me under my cap, and slapped his notebook on his hand. "Well, if it isn't Valentine Beaumont. Hairstylist extraordinaire. Stabs criminals with scissors and pointy combs."

I huffed. "I've never stabbed a criminal with scissors." No need to admit the pointy comb.

He controlled himself from snorting out loud. "What are you doing here? Shouldn't you be at the Wee Irish Dude, breaking open kegs?"

"I beg your pardon?"

"Don't play coy. The whole precinct knows you found that ex-con this morning curled up dead in a beer barrel. Probably be on the six o'clock news."

If I had a dollar for every wisecrack about my involvement in homicides, I'd have enough cash to buy a hundred beer barrels, gold-plated and draped in diamonds. "If you hurry home, maybe you'll get there in time to watch it." Sarcasm at its finest.

He chuckled good-naturedly. "You're one humdinger of a comedian. Always quick with a joke."

"Yes, that's me. Miss Funny Pants. If that's all, officer, I should be going."

"Actually, it's not." His face softened into something I'd never witnessed on hard-boiled Martoli before. "You watch yourself, hear? That nutjob you helped put away is on the loose. I don't want to hear he's harmed you."

I looked over his shoulder, wondering where the real Officer Martoli had gone. I got choked up from his words, and before I could say thank you, he bent and peeked at Tantig. "Lady, more people die in car accidents because they don't buckle up."

Tantig didn't turn to look, but I did catch her eyes roll upward. "Who-hk cares?"

Martoli narrowed his gaze. "What did she say?"

"Uh, she doesn't speak English. Sorry. I'll take care that she buckles up."

"Make sure you do." He yanked up his gun belt and gave a crooked grin. "Seatbelts are for your own safety, lady," he warned Tantig, giving it one last shot.

Tantig pursed her lips. "I'll give you a Tic Tac if you stop talking about seatbelts."

Tic Tacs solved everything as far as Tantig was concerned.

Martoli gave his head a shake like, what was the use? I just wanted to get the hell out of there before he alerted

Romero that he'd stopped me. No sense getting Romero worked up even more by the fact that Max wasn't with me.

"And *you*..." He straightened. "Keep those combs in your bag...and stay safe."

I gave him a nod and rolled up the window. Cops. Who could figure them out?

I ripped off my cap, ogled my hair in the mirror, and decided it looked better now that it had been flattened. I flung the cap in the backseat and drove away, reflecting anxiously on what Martoli had said about Ziggy. True, he was a nutjob. That much was undeniable. But that's not why I was uneasy.

I was uneasy because even cops like Martoli, who normally rolled their eyes at me when they saw me, were worried about my welfare. What did that say? I was doing my utmost to find Ziggy, but if he was too clever for even the cops to catch, we were in trouble. I peered over both shoulders, my nose giving an impulsive twitch. He could be planning one of his clever stunts this very minute.

I tightened my grip on the steering wheel. The bigger problem was that not only did Ziggy know where *I* was, but I didn't have a clue where to find *him*. He could be living under a rock in the woods or staying with friends...if anyone was dumb enough to protect him. He could even be shacked up with a lover, if he had one. Where did I begin to look?

I thought about this some more. Maybe I didn't have to look. Sooner or later, he'd get closer again. He'd left the second creepy message at the salon just a few hours ago. That was two in one day. And he'd only escaped twenty-four hours ago, maybe less. If nothing else, Ziggy was determined. But he'd slip up. Wasn't that what Romero had said? If *he* didn't know, then who did?

I was brought back to the present when Tantig tugged the sleeve of my leather jacket. "You're going to drive right past Kuruc's." Her tone was bland, her demeanor calm. Nothing ruffled Tantig.

I swerved into the half-empty parking lot, found a spot, and helped Tantig out of the car. I flipped up her collar from the cool breeze and hurried her into the store. I shuddered at being out of the cold, then grabbed a cart, and trailed behind Tantig while she hobbled along.

Smells from every country rolled into one delicious aroma that had me salivating as I walked the aisles. As usual, Sam Kuruc, the owner and a jovial guy, had out plenty of samples for people to try. German salami. Italian biscotti. Greek olives. A veritable buffet at any time of day.

Tantig walked on autopilot straight to the grape leaves section, not turning her head once to taste-test anything. Me, I nibbled along the way, convincing myself that food in my stomach would help alleviate my troubles.

I also did the odd over-the-shoulder check and scrutinized the few shoppers who passed by. Men. Women. Kids. I even looked twice at the life-size cardboard cutout of that chef from "Hell's Kitchen."

We were in a fairly empty public place. A deli, for Pete's sake. No one was going to make a move here. I was so confident of this, I even stopped in the juice section to sample a pomegranate punch. Yum.

I threw the paper cup in the garbage, not only keeping my guard up where Stoaks was concerned, but also keeping my eyes peeled for Sam's mother, Hajna the Hungarian witch. I didn't know which would be worse: coming face to face with a convicted murderer or running across the fierce little woman in black with gnarly fingers and buggy eyes.

I tamped down the anxiety at meeting up with either, then accidentally bumped the cart into Tantig while she picked a jar of grape leaves off a shelf. I said I was sorry and backed up a hair, thinking it was my lucky day that Hajna wasn't around.

Tantig put the jar in the cart and pulled a list out of her purse. She mumbled to herself as she perused the list, then poked in her purse again and produced a pen.

All too familiar with Tantig's shopping habits, I opened my bag and scouted around for my tube of gingerbread-scented hand cream. Waiting for her could take time, and my hands needed moisturizing from the raw weather.

I slung my bag back over my shoulder, squirted a dab of cream on my palm, and worked it in, inhaling the rich aroma while putting off notions of soon donning winter gloves. Giving the back of my hand another dose, I turned to the shelves next to me and surveyed the different kinds of olive oils. Virgin. Refined. Tuscan Herb. Garlic. Beside the olive oils were cans of crushed tomatoes, tomato paste, and pasta sauce.

I was studying the various tomato pastes when suddenly, from the other side of the shelves, I heard *ping, ping, ping*. One by one, cans to my right exploded, broken items sailed past my shoulder, and red sauce, oil, and glass flew everywhere.

Before I could grasp what was happening, a gloved hand reached through the shelf and swiped away more goods. A gun was attached to the hand, the tip of a silencer pointed right at me. I stared from the gun up to a Kuruc's brown paper bag covering the thug's head. The bag had two eyeholes and a hole cut for the mouth.

My first thought was that this was a stickup, or worse, a mass shooting. But logic told me a robbery would most likely occur at the checkout where there were cash registers and people paying. Not in the canned goods section. And the silencer on the gun pointed at me assured me this was between the shooter and me. More specifically, Ziggy and me.

It'd been years since I'd seen Ziggy, and I had no idea what he looked like these days. Was he fat? Thin? Stooped over? Muscly from pumping iron? I couldn't tell much from this angle or from the paper bag the gunman was masquerading in. And what if I was wrong? What if this was connected to the case, but it wasn't Ziggy under that brown bag?

My entire body was shaking, and my heart was pounding so fast I was sure I was going to faint. Somewhere in the back of my mind, I was conscious of the continuous hum in the store. The silent shots must not have alerted anyone, and with a store this big, and only Tantig and me in our aisle, it seemed no one else had witnessed the incident. All the better. If the gunman was focused on me, nobody else would get hurt.

The crook's mouth was wide open, and a sneeze came out at me from under the bag, followed by a high, squeaky laugh. "You're going to die."

In a flash, my whole life passed by me. Tears sprang to my eyes and sweat drenched me.

Panicking, I looked from my assailant to Tantig—who was still checking her list—to my trembling hands, back to my assailant. Instinctively, I reached through the shelf, knocked the gun aside, and shot a dose of hand cream into the laughing mouth inside the paper bag.

"*Gaaag!*" The maniac backed away, sputtering and choking on the cream, unable to catch a breath.

I yanked my bag off my shoulder and used it to sweep the rest of the items off the shelf. I needed to get a better look at the shooter. If it was Ziggy, he was dressed in a trench coat, bending up and down, coughing and gagging, the cream doing a good job with clogging his airways. He held onto his paper-bagged head with one hand, gun in the other, then keeled forward and barfed on the floor.

Swiping away my tears, I gave myself a reassuring pep talk that I could catch this lunatic. I told Tantig I'd be right back, then I sucked in deeply for courage, clamped my bag to my side, and hurriedly slid down the row.

By now, employees and shoppers had figured out what was happening, and there was disorder everywhere. Women were screaming. Kids ran amok. Olive and salami trays flew in the air, and people were slipping and falling on top of each other. I couldn't excuse myself past everyone fast enough, and by the time I got to the next aisle, the shooter had fled.

I looked at the puddle of vomit he'd left, then peered to the end of the aisle. Holding back a gag, I asked if anyone had seen where he went. There was so much confusion, everyone pointed in a different direction.

I backed away, stifling nausea, and rushed through the deli. I searched under display tables and over shelves. I bustled into the kitchen, apologized to the staff for my intrusion, and asked if they'd seen the bagged bandit. One employee said someone wearing a brown paper bag and a trench coat had rushed out the front door a minute ago.

I said thanks, turned, and tripped on my heels, hands to the ground. *Fine job, Valentine. How did you expect to catch a crook in four-inch heels?*

Without belaboring the point, I picked myself up, kicked off my shoes, and rammed them in my bag. Then I sped to the front entrance and stumbled past people outside, crashing into a woman who looked vaguely familiar. She apologized and moved aside for me. I didn't stop to ask questions. I was consumed with finding my assaulter. I gave her a brief nod and staggered to the parking lot.

Hopping from foot to foot, the asphalt cold under my feet, I peeked in cars, making sure my attacker wasn't hiding in a vehicle. Nothing looked out of place. Folks were either coming or going, and traffic was moving steadily along the tree-lined street. Nobody was burning rubber, escaping the scene.

I jogged to the back of the building, not thinking I'd find anything there. Except for Kuruc's Dumpster and a few empty cars likely belonging to employees, the area was clean.

I bent at the waist and heaved in air, suddenly feeling lightheaded. I slouched for a couple of seconds, letting the nausea and panic pass. Once I was sure I wasn't going to upchuck or black out, I straightened and took a last glance around. My gaze finally rested on the fully packed Dumpster.

So? It was a garbage bin…where people threw garbage. What did I expect to find? A Versace purse?

Discouraged that I'd let my best chance of finding Ziggy slip through my fingers, I turned to walk away when something caught my eye. It was nothing really. A brown crumpled-up piece of trash stuffed between two black plastic garbage bags. I took another step toward Kuruc's front entrance, but a nagging feeling hauled me back.

Giving in to curiosity, I hiked over to the Dumpster and stared up at the crumpled item. Right. Not exactly in reaching distance, especially in bare feet. I lugged out my heels, slipped on the left shoe, and balanced myself, straightening, four inches taller. Like an acrobat, I reached up with the spike of my right heel and babied the crumpled item toward me.

After it tumbled to the ground, I slid my right shoe on and gently unfolded it with the bottom of my heels. I probably looked like a clumsy hip-hopper, but I wasn't keen on touching the trash with my fingers. And at the moment, I wasn't concerned about appearances.

Once I had it spread out, I knelt and ogled the cutout eyes and mouth, disregarding the fact that I'd retrieved it from a bin that could hold any number of diseases. Bending closer, I smelled remnants of my hand cream mixed with the smell of vomit surrounding the damp area around the mouth.

I leaped to my feet like the item was on fire and did a full body shiver. No doubt this was the bag my assailant had worn on his head. I stared down at it, prickles of dread traveling the length of my arms. What was I to do with this? The police would want to see it, and I had a duty to provide proof that there was a disguised goon trying to kill me.

I wiped my nose with the back of my hand and looked around for something to pick up the soggy bag with. Two things were certain. I wasn't touching it or climbing into the Dumpster in hopes of finding anything useful.

Not coming across anything that would help, I combed through my bag. I had to have something to pluck this garbage off the ground. Pluck? Of course! I could pluck it with my tweezers.

I yanked out my stainless steel, pink-and-orange polka-dot-handled tweezers, nipped the bag off the pavement, and sprinted back into Kuruc's. I needed to make sure Tantig was all right.

I rushed to the section where I'd left her, turned a corner, and came face to face with Hajna.

"*You!*" She poked her gnarly fingers up into my face. "You make this mess in my store."

"*No.*" I jumped back. "There was a madman shooting at me. *He* made this mess." As proof, I held up the bag dangling from my tweezers.

She gawked up at me, unconvinced.

I didn't care what she believed. I knew a madman was responsible for this, and I'd bet anything his name was Ziggy Stoaks. He'd been sending me messages all day. If it wasn't Ziggy, who else could it have been?

Chapter 10

Sam appeared from the meat counter where he'd just hung up the phone. "It's okay, Valentine. Main thing is you're not hurt." He ushered his mother away, looking back over his shoulder. "The police will be here shortly."

In record time, a couple of cruisers squealed to a stop in front of the deli, followed by the ID unit and a TV van. Huh. Maybe Officer Martoli could catch a double feature on the news. I could see the headlines now. BEAUTICIAN CRACKS KEG, THEN CRACKS CROOK.

Lovely.

The crime scene tape went up, and the ID unit unpacked their tool kits and cameras. I ignored all the frenzy and returned to Tantig again. She was in the aisle where I'd left her, looking at items on a shelf that hadn't been shot.

Relieved that the impact of all this hadn't shaken her, I called her name, then slipped in a puddle of oil and crashed, ass to the floor. My head hit the ground with a whack, and the wind got knocked out of me. I lay there almost comatose, staring straight up at the ceiling fans going 'round and 'round.

Tantig rambled over and blinked calmly. "What are you do-ink?"

I rolled my tongue across my teeth, making sure they were all there. "I...uh...thought I saw a big mouse...or a small cat."

"Oh...my...Gaaad." Her tone was flat, her eyes did a half roll.

Being present during a shooting didn't faze her. *This* elicited a dismayed response. Tantig had no use for animals, big or small. In the old country, she claimed, cats and dogs ran rabid, and no self-respecting human paid attention to them, let alone had one for a pet.

I got to my feet, picked up the tweezers and paper bag, and hitched my beauty bag over my shoulder. Then I took a good look at Tantig.

She had globs of oil on her face and hair...and shoulders...and sleeves. And there was a chunk of tomato on her crown. Swell. Wait till my mother saw her. I groaned, not allowing myself to go there. I had bigger issues on my mind.

Tantig stared at the paper bag, unaware she looked like a white goose ready for the oven. "Is that for my groceries?"

I glanced down at the bag. "No. This one has holes in it." Wishing I could see the humor in that, I limped over to our cart, chucked the thing inside, then shoved the tweezers in my black bag.

I brushed the tomato off her head and finished wiping oil off her face when a uniform trooped down the aisle. He escorted Tantig to a cruiser so she could rest while I went through specifics with another officer.

Most of the shoppers had been marshaled out, the last handful offering cops what little they'd seen. I was finishing up my statement when Romero hustled through the doors. He stopped to confer with one of his men who was questioning Sam Kuruc.

Automatically, I ducked, my heart going *pa-bum* at the sight of him, my stomach lurching at the expected reaction when he saw me.

I leaned closer to the shelves and watched Romero pat Sam's shoulder, then take notes from him and the cop. He did some nodding and said a few words to Sam, which brought a look of relief to Sam's face. Then, as if sensing he was being watched, he turned his head and caught my eye.

I leaped back and bashed into the cart, an instant blaze burning through me. A "gotcha" smile curved on his lips. If I were smart, I would've scrammed out the back door, but I was too exhausted to make the effort.

Romero wrapped it up with Sam and the cop, shuffled past several employees and spilled items, and headed my way. His set shoulders and heavy stride said he'd had better days. I wasn't about to argue that…or incidentally bring up his hurt foot.

He paused three feet from me and looked from my head to my toes. I hadn't taken stock of my appearance since the attack, so I took the opportunity and peeked down at myself.

My hair on my shoulders was matted and greasy, my pants were slimy, and my jacket was blotched with tomato goop. Plus, there was an olive stuck to my zipper. Okay, so I didn't look like I was going to the ball.

He plucked the olive off my coat and popped it in his mouth. "You ready to talk to me now?"

Aha. The "gotcha" look. Figured he wouldn't forget about our earlier exchange.

I gulped at the power and size of his mere presence, refusing to let his strength or authority intimidate me. "*Fine*. You're upset with me." I let out a breath, feeling myself getting worked up again. "Maybe I did go to see Luther Boyle. Big deal! You had a lot of nerve asking Max and Jock to watch over me."

"It was for your own protection." His daring blue-eyed stare seemed to look straight into my soul.

I stood my ground, not willing to be sucked in by his good looks or overbearing concern. "In spite of that, what happened here today proves Ziggy's at the bottom of this."

He blew out air. "Nobody's disputing that. But you're like a walking target. Everywhere you go, disaster follows."

"That's not true." I shoved my hands on my hips in defiance. They slid right off from the oil coating me, but the effort was real. "I was at my parents' an hour ago and nothing happened there." I crossed my arms cheekily to seal the point.

He stood cocky-like, hand on his gun hip. "Pardon my mistake."

"You're pardoned." My voice was raspy, which meant I was close to tears...again. But I scrounged up my inner strength and gave him a bold stare.

His face relaxed like he knew he wouldn't get anywhere by playing the tough cop. "Okay. Want to tell me what happened?"

I filled him in on the shooting, not seeing any point in bringing up my actions in self-defense.

After I was done, his gaze took in the whole store, then narrowed on the leaking bottles on the shelves. He glanced at me and back at the shelves. Without a word, he reached his arm past a mess of broken items and retrieved a white plastic tube with orange writing on it.

He sniffed the opening and flicked the lid shut, eyes riveted on me. "Gingerbread."

My cheeks burned. *Damn cream*. Why hadn't I pocketed it?

"Yours?" His voice was deep, steady.

I nodded.

He kept himself in check, but his frustration was evident. "Is there a reason your hand cream was on the shelf?"

"Mmm-hmm."

"Care to let me in on it? Or should I assume we'll be looking for a perp ready for the spa?"

My nostrils flared in anger. "I didn't rub him down with it, if that's what you think."

"I don't know what to think. Please enlighten me."

"I shot it in his mouth," I blurted.

There was a pause, and I hesitantly peeked up into his eyes, waiting for a response. All I got was a raised eyebrow, which highlighted that darn racy scar on his cheekbone.

"It wasn't that bizarre," I argued. "He was wearing a paper bag over his head, and I aimed it at the hole cut out for the mouth."

"A paper bag," he repeated, "with a hole cut for the mouth."

"That's right."

"Did it have holes cut for the eyes, ears, and nose?"

I sliced him a mean look. "Just the eyes."

"Why didn't you shoot him in the eye?"

I gave an innocent shrug. "The mouth was a better target. Then he choked on the cream and threw up."

He angled his head down and rubbed the back of his neck. I couldn't tell if he was grinning or grimacing, so I waited with uncertainty, rolling my tongue inside my cheek.

He lifted his gaze to me in that damn sexy way. "You sure you don't want to ditch hairdressing for a career as a marksman? You'd probably get hired on the spot."

"No, thank you."

I went to snatch the cream, having enough of his sarcasm, but he slid it in his pocket, telling me I'd get it back later. I huffed at that, suddenly remembering flinging the paper bag in the cart.

I spun around and pointed down at the bag. "Said bag. I found it in the Dumpster out back."

He leaned in beside me, hooked the bag into the air with the tip of his pen, and studied all sides of it. "Good work, Tex."

"I only used the cream in self-defense," I continued, feeling the need to explain my actions. "And his gun was pointed at my head."

"I probably would've done the same thing."

I blinked in astonishment. "You would've?"

"No." He placed the bag back in the cart. "I would've fired a gun."

"I don't have a gun, may I remind you."

He choked out a cough. "Good thing. You're too impulsive to own a gun."

I balled my hands into fists. "A moment ago, you said I should be a marksman."

"I've reconsidered. I think archery may be more your style. The kind with those suction cups on the tip of the arrow."

Mr. Hilarious.

He was so close his masculine scent penetrated my senses. But I stood squarely, pretending to ignore the jibe.

He surveyed the mess around us, then squatted and motioned to a chunk of glass. "I have a feeling ballistics will tell us the same gun that shot Dooley also shot these bottles." He gave a head shake. "At least nobody was hurt."

I didn't disagree.

While we were talking about shootings, I dug in my bag and tugged out the red booklet.

Romero stood and took the booklet out of my hand. "What's this?"

"Dooley's journal. He not only took pictures of me, he also recorded his thoughts."

Romero flipped through the book, stopping here and there to read a passage. "So Stoaks wanted Dooley to believe you were his girlfriend."

"Seems that way."

He rapped the notebook in his hand. "It's all starting to make sense. Ziggy holds a grudge against you for putting him behind bars. He meets Dooley in prison. Dooley does his time, and when he's released and headed back to Rueland, Ziggy asks him to keep an eye on you. If he can get Dooley to believe you're cheating on your poor jailed boyfriend, then maybe he can convince Dooley that you deserve to die."

"Sounds about right, now that we know they were doing time together."

He gave me a strange look as if there was no doubt about that in his mind. "But once Dooley starts clicking shots of you left and right, he realizes you're not—nor have ever been—Ziggy's girlfriend."

"Give the man a prize." I was getting my spunk back, showing all kinds of confidence around Romero.

He tapped me on the head with the booklet, giving me a look that all but melted me. "And when Ziggy escaped and hunted down Dooley, they had words that resulted in Dooley's murder."

"That's how I figured it."

Romero slipped the booklet in his pocket, then made a show of stroking his unshaved jaw like something else was on his mind. "You want to tell me where Max is?"

I knew where this change of topic was heading. "He's at Jimmy's…baking bread."

"Baking bread."

"That's right."

He gave me a steady look that I could interpret a hundred ways. But I stayed silent, waiting for him to process this.

"And you were here with Tantig because?"

"She needed grape leaves to make Armenian *sarma*."

He stared at me.

"Little cabbage-type rolls filled with a meaty, rice filling."

He nodded carefully. "And you felt it wise to switch traveling companions from a thirty-year-old fit male to an eighty-year-old woman."

"Max is thirty-one," I corrected.

His stern expression said he wasn't amused.

"Look." I tapped my toe pointedly. "This was supposed to have been a short outing. How did I know Ziggy would come after me in a European deli?"

"Maybe because he's crazy! Because he's a murderer! And *hey*! Just thought of *this* one. Because he's been playing games with you all day! He'll stop at nothing until he kills you." The veins in his neck bulged, and a muscle twitched in his jaw. If I hadn't known better, I'd say Romero was about to blow a gasket.

"Okay already. We still don't know for sure if it was Ziggy. Calm down."

"Calm down!" His arms waved madly, grabbing the attention of the cops in the aisle, dusting and collecting evidence. He speared them a look, and they promptly went back to what they were doing.

"My life was a sea of calm," he said, "until I met you. Now I wake up every day wondering what trouble you'll get into. I haven't worried this much about anyone since…" He paused, and his tone wavered. "In a very long time."

My heart warmed at his confession. He'd gone through a period that had caused him great pain, and I didn't intentionally want to make life worse for him. But I wasn't going to cloister myself away either until Ziggy was caught.

"I'll make a deal with you," I said. "If I suspect any more trouble, if anyone follows me or calls me or sends me any more presents, I'll phone you right away. Okay?"

"This is a small town. I'd hear news about you before you even pulled out your phone." He gripped me by the shoulders, unbothered by the oily feel. Then he whirled us around, away from prying eyes, his voice husky, his stare hungry. "I need you in my life, you know that?"

Without waiting for a response, he dragged me close, bent his head, and gave me a hot-blooded kiss, his tongue possessing mine in a fierce tango.

When we finally broke apart, he stared deep into my eyes. "If calling's the best you can do, I'll take it. Just promise you'll follow through."

I watched him get called away, my legs wobbly from the kiss, my mouth numb.

"Scout's honor." I put my hand to my head and gave his back a woozy two—or was it three?—finger salute.

Chapter 11

It was six-thirty. The wind had calmed down, and the sun had quietly set. Tantig and I had wiped most of the gunk off our clothes, thanks to Sam and the paper towels he'd provided us from aisle four, and we buckled ourselves into my car. Then I called my mother, told her we got held up—no lie there—and were on our way home.

Apart from a killer kiss from Romero, which indisputably was the only good thing that had happened to me today, my day had progressively gotten worse. I was tired of being on guard. Tired of being chased. Tired of being scared. In fact, I'd had enough of this whole game of hunting down Valentine.

Though I wasn't going to broadcast my intentions to Romero, I had to turn the tables and get more active finding Ziggy Stoaks. I was worried he'd get sloppy and accidentally hurt innocent bystanders. If it *was* Ziggy at Kuruc's, he'd already threatened me. What if he'd killed someone? What if he'd hurt Tantig?

I didn't have a clue where to begin looking, and Luther had been no help. But that wasn't going to stop me. I'd caught killers before with little to nothing to go on. This was merely a stumbling block.

Exhaling a pent-up breath, I started the engine, additional thoughts nagging me.

Business, for one. Imagine if Ziggy had slopped paint on the shop window when we were working. Or worse, opened fire there. I couldn't let that happen. I'd lost enough clients due to Phyllis's incompetence. I couldn't afford to lose more because of a crazy escaped felon. I'd have to lock up the shop for good. Walk away in shame. Lose the respect of my colleagues.

It wasn't a pretty picture. If I couldn't afford to work, I wouldn't have the funds to pay the rent on my house. And if I couldn't pay my rent, I'd have to move back in with my parents and Tantig.

I glanced at my great-aunt, tapping Tic Tacs onto her palm.

I love my family, and Tantig made life more colorful, but moving home meant I'd be more susceptible to questions about matrimony and why Romero—or Jock— hadn't asked for my hand in marriage. A high-pitched squeak escaped me at the thought of either man proposing, and the squeak turned into an anxious cough.

"What's the matter?" Tantig asked in a monotone.

"Uh, nothing. Swallowed wrong." I cleared my throat and nabbed a Tic Tac.

It wasn't that I didn't want to be married, but marriage to Iron Man or Hercules was a thought almost too much to entertain. To be honest, Romero and Jock were more superhuman than any other men I'd known. Despite that, Romero and I *had* formally started dating. But my mother liked to pretend she was going on one hundred, and she wanted a ring on my finger before she exited this world.

Before I completely overwhelmed myself with these scenarios, I decided to start at square one on this hellish day.

I shifted my Bug into gear and put on my thinking cap, trying to remember everything that had happened to me since this morning. The answer had to be here somewhere.

First, there was the dildo left on my front porch. Not exactly a waving flag, but not inconspicuous either.

Anyone looking close enough would've noticed it. Maybe one of my neighbors had seen something.

I promised Romero if anyone followed me or sent me any more presents, I'd call. But I never said I'd stop looking for whoever dropped off the dildo, which in the end may lead to the identity of the gunman if, in fact, it was Ziggy.

And though it seemed like Ziggy was the sender, there was something needling me in the back of my mind that this could be wrong. If Dooley had been the source, he would've had to deliver the dildo last night before he was murdered.

I didn't know what time Jimmy had left Dooley alone at the restaurant, but I had a feeling Dooley didn't go anywhere before he was killed at around 10:45. Now that I thought about it, I'd let Yitts out onto the porch for a bit of air at 11:00 before I'd gone to bed, and there was no dildo in sight then. So even if Dooley did have time to leave the restaurant and return by 10:45, he didn't leave anything at my place.

If I was way off base, and it was Candace—the only other suspect I could think of—she would've cruised down the street in her red Corvette, not caring who'd seen her. If nothing else, a red Corvette would be easy to spot.

I contemplated this, pretty sure Candace was a dead lead since everything pointed to Ziggy. She'd also sworn she'd never touched a dildo before...and with Candace's abundant track record with men, this was something I was inclined to believe. Unless she was lying, she was out of the race. Regardless of this, how could I ask any of my neighbors what, if anything, they'd seen?

Mrs. Lombardi, who lived kitty-corner across the street and had a cement statue on her front lawn of the Virgin Mary, would cast me out if I showed up at her door, asking anything about a dildo. Mrs. Calvino, next door to me, couldn't see anything through her perpetual haze of cigarette smoke. And Mr. Brooks? He was like a father figure. It'd be awkward posing anything on the subject.

I crawled out of Kuruc's parking lot onto Darling and made a mental note to at least call my neighbors. I'd deal with the consequences later.

Putting that thought aside, I summoned images of Dooley's body. If there was an inkling of truth to my theory that Ziggy killed Dooley because Dooley wouldn't hurt me, then it was safe to say that Ziggy was nearby, biding his time.

The photos and journal were another matter. Though Dooley had taken a lot of pictures, the shots were all centered around me and places I'd been. There was nothing pointing to Ziggy's whereabouts.

Enter Luther Boyle, state guest at Rivers View Correctional Center. No matter how many times I revisited the conversation with him, I couldn't peg what it was that was niggling me. He was in jail. Ziggy was out. According to Luther, they weren't even that close. Still, I was bothered.

I kept pace with traffic heading toward York Street and the salon, torturing myself again about the drawing on the front window. It had to have been illustrated by the same person who delivered the dildo. He or she had fastened a perm rod around the base of the real apparatus, and the image on the glass was a dead ringer.

According to the kid who worked at Friar Tuck's, he'd been busy serving coffee and donuts and hadn't seen who painted the portrayal. Neither had anyone else. Lots of pictures floating around. None with the artist at work. Just my luck.

This brought me back to the present, surviving a shooting at Kuruc's. I didn't see the face of my attacker, but it had to be Ziggy under that paper bag.

I put these thoughts on the back burner and cranked the wheel to the right, making an impulsive turn into Friar Tuck's lot. Little unknown fact about me: I hate unfinished business. And since the shop-window fiasco left me forgetting to drop off the magazines earlier, I intended to do so before the night was done.

"Where are we go-ink?" Tantig asked.

"I need to take some magazines into the salon. I'll only be a minute, and I think you'd better come in with me."

Tantig raised her chin and gave a *tsk* with her tongue. She could've simply said no, but I caught her drift.

I pulled to a stop behind Beaumont's and patted her hand to remind her of what I'd just said. In the past few hours, I'd been threatened at gunpoint, humiliated, and scared. And my assailant was still out there, waiting for another opportunity to strike. Plus, Tantig had been kidnapped and held hostage on the cruise a mere few weeks ago by the last murderer I'd tried to catch. No way was I going to leave her alone in the car. "Come on, Tantig. I'll help you inside. You can watch the weather channel on my phone while I unload the magazines."

Reluctantly, she agreed. I unlocked the glass door to Beaumont's, helped her up the one step into the salon, threw on the lights, and ushered her into Ti Amo, the closest treatment room to the back door. I perched her on the facial bed, pulled up a video from the weather network on my phone, and showed her how to control the volume. Once I was sure she was comfortable, I slipped back outside and heaved the stack of magazines out of the trunk.

I returned inside again and heard soft snoring coming from Tantig. I peeked in the room and saw her stretched out on the facial bed, fast asleep, my phone resting on her stomach.

Balancing the magazines in one arm, I tiptoed into the room, gently picked up the phone with my free hand, and slid it into my bag. Let her sleep for a few minutes. She'd had a rough day.

I crept out of the room, pulled the pocket door three-quarters of the way closed behind me, and wandered down the hall to the front, the usual mix of chemical and therapeutic smells greeting me. I dropped my bag on the floor by the antique-bronze magazine table and replaced the old magazines with the fresh pile. I cleaned up the reception area a bit and gave a tug on the front door. I knew I'd locked it earlier after Max and I had scrubbed the window, but no harm being extra cautious.

Satisfied the shop was in order, I carted the old mags past the four stations and did a double take at myself in one of the wood-framed mirrors on the wall. *Yikes.* The sight of me almost hurt my eyes. Good thing I was looking at myself from a distance. I probably would've taken the clippers to my hair if I'd gone any closer.

I drew out a groan, marched into the dispensary, and dumped the magazines in the recycling bin.

Just then, I heard footsteps nearing from the direction of the back door. Couldn't be. I locked the back— Oh no! I didn't lock the back door. I'd reentered the shop, focused on Tantig's snoring, and I didn't go back to secure the door. *Blockhead!*

Trying to think positively, my mind raced for a logical explanation of who it could be.

Perhaps Tantig had woken up and decided to wander to the front. Or maybe it was the kid from Friar Tuck's, blessing me with more comments about the cool artwork on the front window. Better yet, maybe Max had wrapped it up at Jimmy's and asked him for a ride home. They could've whizzed by Beaumont's, seen the lights on, and decided to check it out.

Deep down, I knew none of these were likely. Once Tantig was sleeping, nothing would move her. And the Friar Tuck's employee had probably ended his shift around three and gone home, right after Max and I were here. As for the last notion, if Max *or* Jimmy sauntered into the shop, they'd be singing or jabbering or making some other noise. Silence wasn't a strong suit for either of them.

My heart skipped around in my chest, panic mounting by the second. I didn't dare scream for fear that it would alarm Tantig and tip off whoever had entered. I looked around the dispensary for something handy to use as a defense weapon. A French phone. A sturdy broom. Microwave. And a couple of wheeled stools.

The footsteps proceeded down the hall, and terror rose inside me. *Pick something already!*

The last two things were heavy and awkward. I gaped at my pretty, nostalgic phone. Couldn't use *that* as a weapon.

Broom it was!

I clutched the handle with both hands, adrenaline charging through me at such a rate I could barely breathe. I lifted the bristly end over my head and edged past the portable screen in the main salon to the hallway, waiting for my stalker to round the corner.

I was flat against the wall, cursing my stupidity.

The first mistake I'd made upon entering the shop was putting on the lights. If I'd been followed, nothing like holding up a sign.

Second mistake. Right. Unlocked door. *Damn.* Main thing was Tantig had been spared. The intruder might not have even noticed her with the pocket door to Ti Amo almost closed.

I glanced at the front where my bag sat on the floor by the magazine table. *Doh.* Third mistake. Not having any tools on me to protect myself. I tightened my grip on the broom. This would have to do.

A man's boot appeared first in my line of vision, and I didn't wait another second before swinging down and clobbering the perpetrator.

Chapter 12

Before I made contact, I shut my eyes tight, not caring to see if I cracked my assailant's skull, shoulder, or back. The broom was ripped out of my hands, and I was yanked in hard against a firm chest.

I opened my eyes, ready to scream. "*Jock!*"

He looked down into my face. "You were expecting someone else?"

I gave his leather-clad chest a stern whack. "You scared me half to death! How did you know I was standing here?"

"Saw your shadow." He gestured to the floor, then held the broom in the air like it was a toothpick. "What were you planning on doing with this?"

Wiseass. "I was going to clobber you with it."

"Why would you do that?"

"Because I thought you were going to attack me. More specifically, I thought you were Ziggy Stoaks."

He considered this. "Yeah. I could see where you'd think that." He strolled over to the dispensary, leaned the broom against the wall, then turned and raked his gaze over my entire body. I instantly folded my arms across my breasts, the heat from Jock's stare making me feel like I was posing in a lace thong with pasties on my nipples.

He took a step closer, scrutinizing my oil-soaked hair.

"I heard about what happened after you left the prison today."

I gave a thin laugh, thinking about the day I'd had. "You mean the illustration on the front window? Or the shooting at Kuruc's?"

"Both."

Of course he'd heard. It was like an APB had been posted on me and Jock had made it his duty to locate where I was.

He turned his head to the front, then settled his stare back on my face. "You want me to hose down the glass?"

I examined his eyes, trying to guess if this was one of those double entendres he enjoyed employing. *Ooh.* I set my shoulders straight, hiding the fluttering inside. "Max and I did a thorough job earlier. Thanks."

He flung his jacket on a dryer chair, then reached over and gathered my hair in his large palm. "What about you?" In a gentle yet sensual motion, he swept the oily ends behind my shoulders. "You want me to give you a shampoo?"

I gulped back a tremor, remembering what almost took place the last time Jock shampooed my hair. "No, thank you," I rushed out quickly. "I like it this way."

The sexy look on his face told me he remembered the incident, too. More, he didn't believe a word I said. He moved in closer, not hiding the grin creeping in. "You telling the truth?"

I stared up into his eyes, holding back the moan from gazing at the caramel-on-dark-chocolate speckling his irises. "Yes?" I uttered, trying to stay grounded, a challenge around Jock.

He chuckled, then nodded toward the hall. "You know you've got a stowaway sleeping in Ti Amo?"

I spun toward the back. "Tantig!" With Jock strutting in on the scene, I'd forgotten all about her.

"Don't worry," he said. "She's dead to the world."

I peered back up at him. "Would you kindly not use the term...*dead?*"

He leaned against the wall, smiling at my words.

I avoided letting my gaze sweep down his powerful body and refused to admire his seductive pose, both of which would make any healthy female swoon. "What are you doing here, anyway?"

His smile broadened. "Checking to see what time you want me to pick you up tonight."

"Pick me up?"

He folded his arms in front, his tight-knit shirt stretching to accommodate his muscles. "You forget our deal already?"

"Ha." I squeaked so high I hardly recognized my voice.

He moved in and took my hand in his warm grasp, his virile scent weakening my knees. "I believe we shook on it earlier."

I swallowed hard, glancing from his hand that engulfed mine back up into his eyes. I hadn't forgotten my promise about a nighttime ride on his bike. I was simply hoping *he'd* forgotten. Of course, that was like wishing diamonds would fall from the sky.

I slid my hand out of his grasp, Max's remark about riding positions on Jock's Harley popping to mind.

I squeezed my thighs together, attempting to look cool and calm. "In light of everything that's happened today, it's best we rethink this."

His eyebrows went up ever so slightly. "Are you canceling on me, Miss Valentine?"

Tingles spread down my spine at the way he said my name. "*No*." I stepped back from his magnetic aura. "It's just been a harrowing day. All I want is to go to bed."

"I can arrange that, too." He winked.

I forced down a nervous giggle before it erupted from my lips.

"I think you need something to get your mind off today's events." He let that sink in. "Trust me. This will be good for you."

I studied his face, debating the wisdom of his words.

My back still ached from falling hard on Kuruc's floor,

my mind was working overtime on Ziggy's whereabouts, and I was on edge about what my future held. If I toured around Rueland with Jock, it was certain I'd be wrapped in his safety cocoon. No harm would come to me, and that was a soothing thought.

I glanced at the clock. Five minutes to seven. "I have to take Tantig back to my parents' and go home and shower."

He gestured over my shoulder. "I can take Tantig home."

"Ha. You mean on your bike?"

He looked at me. Dead serious.

"It's okay. If my mother knew I let Tantig ride a motorcycle, I'd be skinned alive."

He smoothed the back of his hand against my jawline. "I like your skin the way it is."

Gulp.

He slanted close and brushed his lips across my cheek, his stubble tickling my face. "I'll be at your door, then, by eight-thirty."

I dropped Tantig off at my parents' with the usual amount of aggravation. My father was still bowling, but my mother had enough to say for both of them. Why was I so late? Why was Tantig's hair pink? Why did I bring home two jars of grape leaves?

I crushed the desire to snatch a Turtle brownie cooling on the counter and explained there was a confrontation with a lunatic at Kuruc's. Without going into detail, I told my mother that tomato flew into Tantig's hair, and Sam Kuruc gave me an extra jar of grape leaves to make up for what we'd been through.

I didn't tell her the lunatic had pointed a gun in my face, that I was alive because of the grace of God and a tube of hand cream, and that I'd fallen, hit my head, and seen stars. She could watch the eleven o'clock news for the juicier bits.

"Here," she said after I gave Tantig a hug goodbye, "take some turkey and pilaf home. We've been eating leftovers for days."

She pulled two containers from the fridge and covered the brownies with foil. "And take these brownies. I was going to bring them to the Christmas bazaar, but the church committee told me four dozen squares would be enough." She waved her hand at the kitchen table that overflowed with baked goods. "Guess I overdid it."

My mother baked to the limit when things weren't right in her world. Today, the worry was over me being involved in another homicide. An abundance of squares for the Christmas bazaar was one thing. Baking enough to feed China was another.

I didn't wait around to see what she'd make after she learned the full story on the Kuruc's shooting. I accepted the brownies and the containers of turkey and pilaf, and after a quick kiss on the cheek, I dashed out the door.

By the time I hauled myself into the house, I had pecans in my hair and gooey caramel stuck to my clothes. I'd devoured two brownies on the drive home and was so busy licking my fingers, I didn't see the pothole on Jarvis. What the hell. Add it to the list of goop already glued to me. Heck, add it to the number of things that had gone wrong today.

Without warning, my thoughts shifted to my looming date with Jock. What was I thinking accepting this invitation? I had an escaped convict to catch and evidence to find. I didn't have time to roar around town on Jock's bike like a groupie hanging onto a star. *Darn.* How did I get in these messes?

The kicker was, I couldn't go ten minutes without worrying about my every step. What was Ziggy planning next? And how could I catch him if I couldn't stay ahead of him? Never mind *catching* him, how could I *find* him with the little information I had? He might be crazy, but he was also smart. That meant I had to be smarter.

I slipped off my shoes, threw on all the lights, and took a good look around my modest Cape Cod bungalow. Piano was still standing. Furniture hadn't been touched. Everything else seemed in place. I'd passed a cruiser rolling down my street and felt a certain amount of relief there'd be no surprises once I entered the house. Still, I wasn't as carefree as Rhoda like my mother insisted.

I dropped my bag by the piano and tossed my care packages in the fridge. Then I sloughed out of my jacket and pants, and called for my cat, Yitts. I had an hour to get ready for my adventure with Jock and showering was next, but I wasn't going anywhere without first saying hello to my furry roommate.

Yitts came out from under the couch, stopped in the middle of the living room, and blinked her green eyes at the bright lights. Yawning, she stretched her paws forward on the floor.

"Hard day at the office?" I wasn't about to tell her how *my* day had panned out.

She wove her sleek black body around my bare legs, wanting a snuggle and some food.

I picked her up, gave her a kiss, and inhaled the floral scent of my Musk perfume that seemed to permeate her fur after I sprayed myself each morning. *Ahh.* A breath of fresh air compared to how I currently smelled.

I draped her on my shoulders like a shawl, embracing her warmth.

Out of the blue, the warmth turned to a chill, and I was back at Kuruc's, facing a crazed gunman. Was it Ziggy? Was he responsible for the dildo delivery? The window drawing?

It was like he'd escaped to wreak havoc in my life. Then he'd disappeared into thin air. Had he gone back under the rock he'd crawled out from? Had he stolen a car and fled Rueland?

I tried to think logically where Ziggy was concerned. Only problem was there was no logic to any of this. He was out of control, determined to kill me. Well, he'd almost succeeded. I shuddered, wishing I had a lead so I could send him back to prison and end this insanity.

I puffed out a heavy sigh, hiked into the kitchen, and went for the turkey container. I took a bite of dark meat, ripped off a piece for Yitts, and held it to her mouth. She nosed it for a long moment, probably wondering if something better was coming. She finally ate the morsel but didn't get all happy about it. Yitts wasn't a world-class carnivore. Give her pineapple or cantaloupe, and we'd have something to talk about. I put her down, fed her some niblets, and left her alone to eat.

I went back into the living room, working up my courage to look through my "Rhoda Morgenstern" scarves on my windows at my neighbors' homes. Pulling onto the street earlier, I hadn't thought to note if anything was new in the neighborhood since I'd left this morning. Standing ten feet from the window wasn't going to tell me anything either.

I drew the scarves back and peered outside, letting my eyes adjust to the streetlights funneling down on the homes. I gave Mrs. Calvino's place to the right a quick glance. Only smoke signals coming from her direction. Nothing new there.

Several neighbors had put out their garbage for tomorrow. *That* was new since this morning. Mr. Brooks, across from me, had burlap tied around a small evergreen near his front door. *That* was new. As was the kid's bike left on the lawn four doors down. Yet none of this told me anything vital about Ziggy or the dildo.

I peeked to the left at Mrs. Lombardi's. It was in darkness. But that didn't mean a thing. If I traipsed across the street and rapped on her door, she'd rip it open like she'd been standing there all along. Heck, she was probably looking at me through her binoculars right now.

I leaped back from the window at that thought and dimmed the lights.

A quiver went through me as I pondered asking Mrs.

Lombardi anything. Maybe I'd call Mr. Brooks first. I tiptoed back to the window and saw that his living room light was still on.

I plopped onto the black beanbag chair and grabbed the handset off my Pooh phone.

"Sorry, dear," Mr. Brooks said. "There must be a bad connection. I thought I heard you say you had a dildo delivery."

After an awkward few minutes of conversation, it was apparent Mr. Brooks hadn't seen a thing. I tried Mrs. Lombardi next and got a sermon from the mount. No answer as to whether she'd seen anything suspicious this morning when she walked her poodle, Chester. Just self-righteous condemnation on my predicament.

I called Officer Ray Donoochi and a few other neighbors but came up empty when I mentioned this morning's delivery. It was Sunday, after all. Mass for some. Sleeping in for others. At least Ray promised he and his teenage sons would keep a lookout. This provided some comfort. Jake and Leo were strong, tough boys who'd come to my rescue before.

It was a tossup whether I'd bother with Mrs. Calvino. I didn't know much about my smoky neighbor except she was divorced, had grown children, and supported tobacco farms. She spent most of her days tarring up her lungs on her front porch. When it got too cold out, she moved the party inside.

I dialed her number anyway. What could it hurt? No one else was any help.

Dragging out a cough, she told me she didn't get out for her morning ritual today because her son had delivered an air purifier first thing.

I asked if I could speak to her son. Maybe he'd seen something when he arrived at her house. She agreed and told me Dom worked at Lumber Mart. Best to visit him there since he'd rather she didn't hand out his number. I thanked her and made a mental note to visit Dom first thing in the morning.

Grateful that I had somewhat of a lead, I dialed Max next.

"I'm spending the night at Jimmy's," he said.

I coiled the phone cord around my finger. "What for?"

He let out a rueful sigh. "This bread-baking business is no easy job. We made a nice loaf today, but it took forever to understand the machine. Now that we think we've got it, I want to make pizza dough tomorrow morning."

"If you're sure…" Not that I was looking for an excuse to postpone my date with Jock, but I did promise I'd take Max home.

"I'm sure. It'll probably be noon before we're done." He paused, and I sensed we were moving on from pizza dough. "When is your big night on that exotic machine?" His tone was mischievous. "And I don't mean on the Harley."

I didn't want to get Max going again on Jock's intentions or delve into what had happened to me today at Kuruc's, so I told him my ride was tonight and we'd talk tomorrow.

"Keep me posted," he said. "I want updates."

I hung up, jumped in the shower, and washed my hair. Once I smelled pretty again, I brushed my teeth, fixed my makeup, put on new earrings, and slipped into jeans, a light-weave turtleneck, and suede boots. No time to fuss with my hair, so I swept it to the side and wove it into a loose braid.

I didn't think I was looking forward to this outing. But riding into the night with the wind on my face seemed like the perfect antidote for this horrible day. Maybe the crisp air would give me a fresh outlook on life. Maybe the ride would offer clues to help solve this case.

I had five minutes to spare before Jock arrived, so I sat at the piano in the living room and flipped open the lid. After rotating my shoulders and cracking my knuckles, I hammered out a classical piece.

The fear and frustration I'd endured today worked itself from my neck, down my arms, and out my fingertips. The harder I pounded the keys, the calmer I felt.

Suddenly, there was a curt knock on the door. I screamed bloody murder, clapped a hand to my heart, and flung the piano lid down. *Whew!* So much for being calm.

I took a deep breath, got myself under control, then strode to the front window. Jock was a few minutes early. Couldn't say the same thing for him at work since he came and went like the wind, so this was impressive.

I cocked an ear for my wind chimes that had been tinkling in the breeze. But they'd come to a complete halt. No clinking. No jingling.

I peeked outside, a tingle spreading through me in anticipation. But it wasn't Jock standing on my porch.

Figured. Next to God, there was only one person who had the power to intimidate wind chimes. And he was standing on the other side of the door.

Chapter 13

I'd barely swung the door open when Romero hooked his arm around my waist, lifted me an inch off the ground, and pulled me flat against his rough leather jacket and hard, rugged body. He planted his full lips on mine, his irresistible masculine smell wrapping itself around me, his bristly beard scratching my cheek.

I abandoned any prior thoughts and embraced the kiss, the heat from his burning hunger moving through me like liquid fire. His tongue spiraled expertly around mine, seizing my mouth, fueling the yearning inside. He deftly slid his hands down my back, clasped my buttocks, and molded me closer. No mistaking he was turned on.

He sucked on my bottom lip for a fervent moment, then tore himself away, his mouth hot, his stare intense. "You're a sight for sore eyes."

His fingers grazed my rhinestone earring, and he moved in again, his voice almost a hush as he planted a soft kiss just below my ear. "They say diamonds are forever."

An ardent rush ripped through me from his stroke that was stimulating yet tickled my skin. I gripped the doorframe, my heart thumping from the kiss, my feet struggling to support me. "You have any more clichés you want to share?"

"Only one." He drew me in for another squeeze. "You looked like you needed that."

"Like *I* needed that!" Actually, he was right. I did need soothing, just not in the arousing way Romero offered. At any second, Jock would be at the door. Not that I cared what he thought, but I didn't want to be caught with my pants down...so to speak.

"And I don't think that's a cliché." I peered down at his muscular neck and opened collar, dampening the desire to rake my fingers through the dark hair on his chest and pull him in for another long kiss. "And you're pretty sure of yourself, detective."

He gave me a roguish grin, his gaze dropping to my breasts. He took his toned hands and skimmed them down my sides, his thumbs subtly brushing my nipples through my thin sweater.

"Would you rather I torment you by flickering my tongue on your hot skin?" His voice was low, husky with longing.

Oh Lord. My breasts tingled, and I was almost comatose with pleasure. An aura of brazen sex appeal surrounded Romero. He knew it, too.

I groaned, all thoughts of Jock and clichés vanishing, the throbbing inside me from Romero's touch nearly sending me into orbit. If I didn't break free, I'd have an orgasm here and now.

I mustered what strength I had left and wriggled out of his grasp, the power of his kiss leaving me weak and shaky. "How do you do it?"

"Do what?" He closed the door behind him and followed me into the living room.

"Cope when there's so much misery out there."

He slapped my butt. "It helps when you have something to look forward to."

I jumped and turned around, catching his penetrating stare on my figure. Suddenly, I remembered his words this morning about wanting me in one piece because of things he had planned. And by the look in his eyes, he didn't mean making bread. "Uh, did we have something on for tonight?"

"Not in a formal sense." His eyes darkened, the spark there sexy and dangerous. "But you've been on my mind all day."

The man headed a tight unit of tough cops and was in demand 24/7. Where did he get the sexual appetite?

My cheeks heated, the implication of his words sending a fiery pulse to my groin. Dating Romero was still in the early stages, and if I wasn't careful, I'd forget my oath to take it slow and I'd rip off his clothes with my bare teeth.

I gulped, reining in my thirst. "Why don't you tell me what you've learned about Ziggy?"

He grinned, not fooled by my ploy. "Okay. You win. What do you want to know?"

I shrugged. "Any news on his whereabouts? The journal? The shooting at Kuruc's?"

"Negative on his whereabouts." He spread his jacket wide, his gun gleaming at his hip. "But forensics is working on matching the saliva from the paper bag. I'd bet my pension it was Stoaks under that crude mask. Plus, a Buick was hot-wired shortly after the Kuruc's episode and ditched in the south end of town. No fingerprints on the car, but hair samples from the driver's seat should match samples from the paper bag our boy wore."

"So if it *is* Ziggy, he's still around." I narrowed my eyes, calculating where he'd strike next.

"As for the journal," he continued, "we matched the handwriting to some of Dooley's paperwork from the Wee Irish Dude." He gave me a nod. "You were right about him. He agreed to stalk you, then realized you weren't the girlfriend Stoaks claimed you to be. The last entry in the journal contained several expletives showing remorse and shame, and an oath that Dooley was washing his hands clean of Stoaks."

A trace of sadness filled me again when I thought about Dooley dying because he refused to hurt me. Maybe he'd started out tracking me for Ziggy, but in the end, he'd done the right thing.

I chewed on my lip and frowned.

Romero's breathing slowed, and his eyes dilated. "You keep chewing on that lip of yours, and I'm going to have to do something about it." He took a step closer when the sound of a loud engine rumbled down the street. A moment later, the noise died in my driveway.

Romero looked at the window. "You expecting someone?"

I swallowed carefully. "Um, Jock?"

He did the cop stance, his shoulders tense. "You don't seem too sure about that."

"I'm sort of sure…since we have a date."

"A *date*."

"Not a *date* date. More like a bike-ride…date."

"A bike ride. At nine o'clock at night. With Mr. Universe." His hands were on his hips as if he didn't know what to make of this.

I clutched his wrist, peeked at his Iron Man watch, and smiled up at him sheepishly. "It's only eight forty-one… and a half."

He stared down at me, stone cold, the lines around his mouth tight.

"Well, it's your fault!" I stammered. "You were the one assigning half of Rueland to watch out for me."

"And that's what he's supposed to be doing…watching out for you." It was more a clarification than a question.

Before I could answer, there was a knock on the door. Romero gave me a stern look, then strode over to the door and opened it.

Jock dominated the doorframe, dressed in a black leather jacket and pants and snakeskin boots. The same boots he'd worn not two hours ago when he'd stepped foot in the salon. And if I hadn't been such a dope, I would've recognized his boots the second I'd seen them. A shiver ran through me. Okay. So I'd acted impulsively. *He could've been a killer.*

Jock inhaled deeply, probably debating entering the house. He nodded at Romero, keeping a grin in check that showed he'd heard our exchange. The high-voltage tension between the men bounced off the walls like a ricocheting bullet.

I didn't know what the problem was. A mere twelve hours ago, they were standing in Jimmy's restaurant, discussing Dooley's death. What was so different now? Because the focus was off Dooley? Because they were on my turf? Because they both had feelings for me? There was a moment's pause where they were alone with their thoughts, then Jock tilted his head at Romero.

"Any news on Stoaks?"

"No *good* news." Romero's chin hiked up a notch, and his hand rested on his gun hip. It wasn't a huge statement, but the pose suggested who was in charge here, and more importantly, who was the love interest. His phone vibrated. He tugged it out of his pocket and read the screen. "Got to go. Job's calling."

There was an unmistakable gleam of triumph in Jock's eyes. If I hadn't known better, I'd say he was looking forward to getting me alone.

My insides did a loop-de-loop, and I couldn't determine if it was out of anticipation of the night or worry. Jock caught my eye and winked, and I knew the nervousness was *both* from anticipation and worry.

I put my shoulders back, pretending to ignore his seductive wink. I was a woman in control. Having two men in my house raging with testosterone, each of them extremely handsome *and* sexy, didn't have any effect on me. No siree.

Romero sauntered to the door, clearly doing his best to mask the pain in his foot. He turned and straightened to his full six feet. "You going to be okay?" His eyes softened as he gazed down at me.

"Yep," I squeaked, gripped by the devotion I saw in his eyes.

He looked back up at Jock. "She's not a fan of bikes. Take good care of her."

Jock gave Romero an assertive nod, the gesture saying he wasn't the least bit threatened by another man, detective or otherwise. "I plan to."

Romero gave me another kiss, full on the lips, then slammed the door behind him.

We were on the road ten minutes when Jock swerved off Montgomery and headed south toward Lexington. I leaned into him, holding on for dear life, switching from closing my eyes tight to opening them wide so I could catch a glimpse of the nighttime scenery.

We zipped by Phyllis's neighborhood, flew by the Cotton Gin—the old fabric warehouse—and crossed over ancient railway tracks that were covered knee-high with weeds. None of this was awfully scenic, and I was beginning to think this whole idea was a bust.

I didn't have a clue where we were heading, and I'd changed my mind about the crisp air and fresh outlook on life. It was damn cold out. Despite being swaddled in my leather jacket and sitting behind Jock who made a decent windbreaker, I was almost at my limit of touring the town on a motorcycle.

Jock slowed down to avoid a rough patch in the road, and I told myself I was acting like a spoiled brat. He had something planned, and I'd have to trust him. I sucked it up, buried my head into his back, and prayed we'd get there soon.

We traveled a few more miles, then Jock curved onto a single-lane paved road boasting a sign that said Rueland Area Airport. We sailed past the sign, and I tapped his shoulder.

"I think you made a wrong turn," I shouted into the headset. "That sign said Rueland Area Airport."

Jock took his hand off the handlebar and squeezed my leg. "You don't have to yell. I can hear you clearly."

I wasn't yelling because I didn't think he could hear me. I was yelling because I was freaking out. "What are we doing at an airport? We're supposed to be going for a bike ride."

He patted my leg and resumed his grip on the handlebars. "We are. Having fun yet?"

The stars were out by the millions. The end of my braid was flying in the wind. Reluctantly, I had to admit that for the first time in twelve hours, I'd left the trauma of the day behind. Of course, that was probably because I couldn't think straight since my hands were frozen and my brain was numb from the cold.

I kept my arms tightly wrapped around Jock's waist. I was too afraid to loosen my grasp even though we'd parked near a two-story building and Jock had killed the engine.

He helped me off the bike and released my bag from one of the saddlebags by the back wheel. Then he set our helmets inside the carriers where they were safe.

"What are we doing here?" I swung my bag over my shoulder and rubbed feeling into my hands.

"Part two of our date." He gestured to the hangar where a small plane and a helicopter sat out front on the tarmac.

I gaped, my gaze moving from the hangar, to the red windsock on a pole blowing in the wind, to the airstrip lined with red and blue lights.

"Part two?" I shot him a chilly glance. "You never said anything about a part two."

He took my hand and led me toward the hangar. "Thought I'd surprise you."

"With what?"

"A chopper ride over the city."

I stopped cold and pulled back. "I think I'll be going now."

He chuckled and gripped my hand again. "You haven't lived until you've seen Boston at night."

"I've seen Boston plenty of times at night." I yanked away from his grasp and was getting so worked up I flapped my hands like I was taking flight myself. "We watched a Red Sox game not that long ago, if you remember." I stalled for time. "In fact, I was just in Boston last week. For a pap test. By the time I walked back to the garage, paid for my parking, and wound my way through traffic jams out of the city, it was pitch black. Woo-hoo. See? I've seen Boston at night. No need to fly over the city."

"You haven't seen it like this." He wasn't taking no for an answer.

He towed me several feet, and I put on the brakes again, wondering how he'd set this up. "Is this chopper person another one of your acquaintances, like the warden at Rivers View? Some guy you did stunt work with?"

His face went blank. "No. I simply phoned the airport and booked a ride. But since you mentioned it, Alan, the pilot, did do a stint in the military."

Of course.

"Listen, I should really be home, putting the missing pieces of this case together…for Jimmy's sake. I mean, aren't you the least bit concerned that justice is served for Dooley? That we catch Stoaks and prove he's the murderer?"

He took his large, well-defined hand and tipped my chin up so he could look directly into my eyes. "I'm more concerned about you." He glanced over his shoulder at the hangar, then gazed back down into my face. "I won't force you to do anything you're not comfortable with." He stroked my jawline. "You know that, right?"

Arousal dipped down my spine, summoning the memory of our night together on the ship…and the morning after. *Cough.* Jock was sexy, tempting, and alluring. And not once had he pushed himself on me. *Darn.* How could I fight a man when he was being gentle and considerate? That was even *more* of a turn-on.

When I thought about the things Jock had done with his life, a helicopter ride over the city was probably the tamest. I took a couple of deep breaths and calmed myself. If Jock could do it, I could put on my big-girl panties and do it, too. I'd just ridden on the back of a Harley, for crying out loud. I'd survived *that* chopper ride. How much worse could this one be?

Chapter 14

We entered the hangar and met Alan. He told another guy who was working on the tail of a glider plane that he was taking us up. Then he led us out to the helicopter pad. After he and Jock spoke legalities, he ushered us into our seats, handed us headphones, made sure we were properly buckled in, and slid into the cockpit directly ahead of me.

I looked front to back and side to side, my palms sweaty, my mouth dry. It wasn't a huge chopper, and it wasn't tall. Not only had we needed to duck under the propellers when boarding, but the inside appeared even more snug. Too snug.

My heart seemed to swallow itself, and I couldn't breathe. Last thing I needed was a panic attack. I told myself to think happy thoughts. Forget I was about to fly in a sardine can. Absolutely. I could do this.

I angled forward, curious about the dozens of switches, dials, and buttons on the instrument panel. *Holy moly.* This wasn't helping. Governor light? Hydraulic system? Manifold pressure? I knew a little about *blood* pressure since mine was evidently rising, but what the heck did manifold pressure and the other things mean? And who would fly this thing if something happened to Alan?

I peeked to my right at Jock. He'd been in the navy,

traveled the world, and probably knew all about aircrafts. Whew. What was I worried about? "You ever flown a helicopter before?"

He grinned. "You mean was I trained to man the anti-torque pedals, collective control, and throttle?"

"Yeah. That."

"No."

"*What?* What did they teach you in the navy if you didn't learn how to fly a chopper?"

He leaned over me, brushed his fingers across my breasts, and gave the seatbelt a firm tug. "How to work under stress, how to be loyal, how to be a minimalist." He waited a beat until I stared up into his face. "How to make eye contact when speaking."

My eyebrows jerked so high they almost reached the band on my headphones. "What good is making eye contact when your plane is going down?"

He gave a deep laugh that almost matched the pounding of my heart. "You'd be surprised."

I gaped at him. "Let me get this straight. You speak a dozen languages, you're a master-at-arms, and you've done all kinds of stunt work. Yet you can't fly a helicopter." I shook my head in disgust. "Remind me not to give you the Purple Heart for bravery."

"You mean the Medal of Honor."

I made a tight line with my lips. "Yeah. That's what I mean."

Alan spoke into his headset to someone at the other end about cyclic friction, tail rotor, and trim control. It all sounded like gibberish to me, unless cyclic referred to biking, rotor meant sailing, and trim involved sewing. But in part of my brain—the part that didn't understand mechanical things—I knew my guess was way off. This was aviation talk, and the only thing I did understand was that the tank was full of fuel. Thank God for that.

"Ready?" Alan smiled back at us, then pushed and held a white starter button. Swiftly, the engine roared to life, and overhead, the propellers wound up.

My throat went tight, and my heart knocked so loud, the *waft-waft* from the propellers dimmed in comparison. I looked heavenward to say a short prayer and spotted a fire extinguisher sitting above our heads.

Fresh panic set in. Why was there a fire extinguisher? Were fires common in the cockpit? Were we going to crash? Oh boy. What had I gotten myself into?

Logically, I knew Jock had been a firefighter in the navy, but what good would that do when we were burning in midair? And how would one tiny fire extinguisher save us when we'd all die from a crash landing?

I tapped Alan's shoulder. "Where's the nearest hospital?"

He gave me a sideways glance. "Eight point five miles." He grinned. "You asking out of curiosity or concern?"

"Both."

Jock slipped my hand into his. "This will be fun. You'll see."

In that instant, I thought about Max's wisecrack about riding Jock's bike. I wished that was *all* the fun I was dealing with at the moment.

We went straight up, and Jock gave my hand a gentle squeeze. "You'll get more out of it if you open your eyes."

"They're open. They're looking inward instead of outward."

I could feel him smiling next to me. "The main goal of this excursion is to look outward."

I took a second to inhale and exhale, then squinched my eyes open.

Jock was right. The view was spectacular. Winding roads. Colorful lights. Neighborhoods. Forests. There was too much to look at to worry about nerves. My heartbeat settled into a steady pattern, and Jock's warmth reassured me.

Within minutes, we approached a white halo surrounding a city. The bright lights of Boston. We flew over the John Hancock Tower, Quincy Market, and TD Garden. The city was alive with action, from sports nightlife, to the theater district, to bumper-to-bumper traffic. We swooped over the Zakim Bridge and wowed at the reflection of the city lights on the Charles River.

Jock massaged his thumb across my hand and spoke into his headphone. "Special, isn't it?"

Words wouldn't come for the tears in my eyes. I lugged my bag onto my lap and scrounged around for my phone.

"What are you doing?" Jock asked.

"Max wanted an update on where we went." I fumbled with my phone but managed to get a few shots I could show Max.

Before I knew it, we were heading back to Rueland. A hollow pang gripped my heart at leaving the dazzling lights of the city behind, but I was enjoying the ride too much to feel letdown.

Alan explained landmarks as we neared the south end of Rueland: parks, churches, powerlines. He swerved to the right and pointed to a long one-story building. "That's the last one before landing."

Jock and I both tipped to the side to see what he was talking about. "What is it?" I asked.

"An abandoned puppy mill. Guys who ran it went to prison for murdering some dog groomer a few years back." He shook his head. "I'd be glad to see the place burned down."

My eyes got huge, and I forced down a swallow. Suddenly, it hit me what had struck a chord earlier with Luther. He'd mentioned the puppy mill that he'd run with Ziggy. Maybe it was abandoned like Alan said. But I didn't believe it. This had to be it. This was where Ziggy was hiding out. I snapped a picture of the building and dropped my phone in my bag, anxious to get on land.

"What was that shot for?" Jock asked. "A keepsake?"

I stabbed my finger back toward the puppy mill. "That's where Ziggy's hiding."

"What?" He blinked like he hadn't heard right. "How do you know that?"

I exhaled with a tad of impatience. "Facts. We know Ziggy's been taking cover nearby since escaping prison last night. First, there was the dildo delivered to my doorstep. Then the painted shop window. And it's almost certain he was the gunman at Kuruc's. He *has* to be staying somewhere close."

Jock grimaced. "Okay. Say that's all true and Stoaks is the culprit. That doesn't prove he's hiding in the old puppy mill. I've been by there before. It's all boarded up. Trust me. No one's living there."

Alan gently lowered us onto the tarmac. Once we touched ground, I swiveled back to Jock. "The police think Ziggy stole a car after the shooting and ditched it in the south end of town."

"So?"

"This is as south as Rueland gets. If he's not here, where else could he be?"

"I like your logic." He flicked the tip of my chin.

"Well?"

"Well, what?"

"Are we going to drive by the puppy mill? Check it out?" I was almost on top of his lap, impatient with the prospect of capturing Stoaks.

Alan pressed a button that cut the engine and wound down the propellers. He helped us out of the helicopter and aimed for the building. "It's none of my business," he said, turning, "but there's been no action at the puppy mill for years. Like I said, it'd be better to burn the place down."

"Thanks, Alan." Sheesh. Like his word was gospel because he flew a helicopter over a building now and then.

Jock arched an eyebrow at me. "You just dismissed the guy."

"Did not!"

"Did too." He shook his head. "Maybe you should take someone's advice once in a while."

"What, because he flies in and out of here all the time? That makes him an expert on the puppy mill?"

"Yes!" He stood, legs apart, hands on hips. "Now that you've insulted the guy, I've got to go in there and pay him for giving you the ride of your life."

I jutted my chin forward in defiance, ignoring how sexy he looked, dressed in black leather, his brown shoulder-length hair blowing in the wind. "I'm grateful for the ride. And I'm sorry if I was short with Alan. But it's not him *or* you who's getting dildo deliveries and being shot at. And if you don't want to take me three hundred feet to see what's up at that building, then that's okey-dokey with me." I'd just do it on my own. I planned to get more active finding Ziggy Stoaks anyway, right? I didn't need Jock de Marco's help.

Tomorrow was Monday, and the shop was closed. I'd come back then.

Jock gave me a penetrating stare, as if he was trying to read my thoughts. The stare zinged me right to the core, but I wouldn't cave. Maybe I did speak out of turn, and maybe I was a bit on the stubborn side, but this was something I was willing to bet my life on.

I bared my best poker face, and he blew out a sigh that all but said he gave up. Then he turned on his heel and trucked to the building, the fading echo of his boots on the tarmac leaving a pit in my heart.

I watched Jock disappear, then hauled my phone out of my bag again. "Don't worry about me," I shouted to no one in particular. "I'm going to call Romero."

"Need rescuing already?" Romero said when I dialed him. Cheeky.

"Not quite." I imagined Iron Man rescuing me from Hercules. Wouldn't that be a sight to see?

"What's up?"

I tucked away my absurd thoughts and waited for a moment while a plane engine stopped and started in the background. "I found where Ziggy's staying," I shouted into the phone.

"What do you mean you found where he's staying? Where are you?"

"Rueland Area Airport."

"What?" He wasn't exactly hollering, but he wasn't exactly calm. "What the hell are you doing at the airport?"

I rolled my eyes at his reaction, then put my back to the aircraft rumble. "Relax. We went for a helicopter ride over Boston."

"Oh. Perfect. Now I can put my feet up and have a cigar."

"Is that sarcasm?"

"I'm trying not to let it be." He took a moment like he was thinking this through. "Why were you flying over Boston?"

"It was Jock's idea. And before you ask where he got the idea, he simply wanted to relax me after the horrendous day I had."

"I could've relaxed you without you leaving the ground." His voice took on an intimate tone, and I could almost see the predatory look in his eyes.

I turned up my collar from the wind gusting around me, deciding to make this short. "About Ziggy's whereabouts…"

I heard a whack like he'd bashed into his desk, followed by the squeaky sound his chair made when he parked himself in it. "Damn *drawer*." Another whack. This time as if he'd slammed it shut.

I chose to play it smart and refrain from saying anything. It hadn't been an easy day for Romero either. On top of a sore foot—compliments of yours truly—and another murder case with few leads, I had an inkling he was put out because of my night with Jock.

"Okay." He released one of his aggravated sighs. "So you know where Stoaks is staying. Want to let me in on the secret?"

"It's not such a big secret. It's the old puppy mill by the airport."

"What? Forget it. Nobody's there."

"Not you, too. Everyone seems to think the place is abandoned."

"Who's everyone?"

"Alan. Jock."

"Alan?"

"The pilot. He said there hasn't been any action there in years."

"He's right. And if he's flying over the place on a regular basis, he'd know. I'm ticked I didn't think of that myself. I could've saved the manpower."

I pressed my phone closer. "What manpower?"

He took a heavy breath. "I had a couple officers investigate the puppy mill."

"When?"

"Today."

I straightened, my bag squeezed to my side. "When today?"

Papers rustled at his end. "You want an exact time, Chief, or will a rough estimate do?"

I squinted into the phone and made a face. "Doesn't matter. Forget I asked."

"Yeah, right. Upon learning of Ziggy's escape, I had some uniforms check it out first thing this morning. I figured there was a possibility he'd revisit his old haunt. But I was wrong. There were no signs of life on the grounds. Everything's been boarded up. Locked. Abandoned."

Hmm. "Okay. You win."

"Does that mean you'll let go of this idea?"

How could I argue facts with Romero, Jock…and Alan? "Consider it stricken from my brain."

"Hmph."

I couldn't remember Romero ever using a *hmph* on me before. Hearing him mutter it now sounded unnatural, skeptical. Well, I wasn't going to stand here and worry about what he thought. I said I'd strike it from my brain, and I meant it.

Of course…if something happened to make me think otherwise, I'd simply alter my course of action. That was a woman's prerogative, wasn't it?

After telling me to stay close—but not too close—to Jock, he hung up.

I pitched my phone in my bag, meditating on Romero's news. If Ziggy wasn't hiding in the old puppy mill, then where was the creep?

I was summoning ideas when a right arm came around my neck and forced me back against a solid body. My bag was ripped from my arm and tossed on the ground. A second later, I saw the edge of a straight razor right before it was pricked under my chin.

"Scream, and I'll slit your throat."

I could barely hear the soft voice at my side for the howling wind, the plane engine in the distance, and blood rushing through my ears. Somewhere in my subconscious, I was trying to determine if the voice was the same one I'd heard at Kuruc's. There was nothing I could do to confirm my suspicions, but it didn't matter. The trench-coat sleeve under my chin that I'd seen sweeping the shelf of items at the deli told me Ziggy was my captor.

"How do you like it, hmm? Not so nice having a hair tool threatening you." Despite the background noise, his soft voice once again sounded unnatural to me.

His trench coat flapped around my legs. The razor's steel edge scraped my skin. His grip was strong, making it hard to breathe, let alone find words. All that came out was a whimper.

"This ain't nothing compared to where you're going to feel this blade next." He lowered his razor hand to my groin, nudging me suggestively. "Tit for tat, shall we say."

Fear hurtled my heart into my mouth. After all these years, Ziggy was finally making good on his promise to get back at me for maiming him and sending him to jail.

He towed me toward the woods, and I knew without a doubt if I screamed, he'd slice me on the spot.

My nails bit into my palms, my mind racing with

horrible thoughts. Wait! Where was Jock? How long did it take to pay for a chopper ride? My gaze swept the dimly lit area, hoping he'd materialize.

Maybe I could keep Ziggy occupied until Jock showed up. Oh boy. Who was I kidding? Once other males met Sir Worldly, they got all chummy, asking him questions about his diverse past, boasting about their own scrawny muscles in an effort to measure up.

Face it, Valentine. You're on your own. I gurgled back hysteria, scanning the area again. I had to escape this lunatic, but how? Ziggy wasn't a big man, but he was still bigger than me. And without my tools, I felt weak and outmatched.

Tears filled my eyes, the reality of my situation torpedoing me in the stomach. I shivered, the chill in the night air multiplying my fears as Ziggy dragged me away from the helicopter pad. My gaze fell to my bag ten feet away, and I choked back a desperate cry.

I was going to be brutally tortured and die cold and alone, and I wouldn't even have a lousy hairbrush to fend off my killer. I felt woozy from the images I was conjuring up of my bloody, dismembered body, not found for days…maybe weeks.

I forced myself to snap out of it. I envisioned Dooley's slight, lifeless form curled up in a broken beer keg. He'd been murdered and had no one to speak for him. That wasn't going to be me. Dooley needed a voice, and so did I.

I sniffed back tears, a surge of determination swelling inside. I wasn't going to be another murder victim and let Ziggy carve me up and leave me for dead in some forest beside a small-town airport. I'd been beaten and come close to death before, and in those weakest moments I realized I had the strongest will to live.

I squirmed in Ziggy's arms, digging my heels in the ground while a plan formed in my mind. "Let me wipe my eyes," I cried. "My mascara's burning and blinding me."

"What the *hell*?" He stopped in his tracks.

"It'd be a lot easier for you if I wasn't writhing in pain." I squirmed again for emphasis.

"Geez, you're a pain in the ass. I heard you were a Type A, but this takes the cake." He jolted me up to keep my legs from buckling under me. "You're going to be dead in a few minutes. What does runny mascara matter?"

I blinked like a madman, which I was close to becoming, pretty sure my tears were doing a bang-up job of smearing my makeup. "I can't see!" I wailed, sniffling and sobbing, then cut it at once in outrage. "Who said I was a Type A?"

"*Everyone!* Brother. You're not exactly a recluse. Every time I turn around, you're in the news."

"So?" I thrashed around some more, trying to get him to loosen his chokehold. "Being in the news doesn't make me a Type A!"

"You're impatient, strictly organized, and anxious. If that isn't a Type A, I don't know what is." He secured my wriggling. "And you're a control freak. That's from my *own* observations."

"I am *not* a control freak!" I yelled, attempting to get control of the situation.

He held on tight, his voice rising furiously. "You had control of that perm rod you wrapped around my bangers."

"That's because you were going to stick me with a knife," I retorted angrily. "And I don't appreciate you talking vulgar to me." Yowza, fear was making me nervy.

"You really are something," he said. "Excuse me for not using the proper term."

I coughed and blubbered and sniffed, adding some moaning to the mix. It must've been appalling because I felt him loosen his grip.

"All right, all right already." He produced a tissue, probably from one of his trench coat's many pockets, and waved it in my face. The razor was firm in hand, his right arm still around my neck. "Try anything funny, and I'll cut you open right here."

My nose was running, my cheeks wet, and I could taste salty tears on my tongue. I snatched the tissue from his hand, wiped my eyes, and gave my nose a good honk.

"*Geez.*" He shook his arms away from me and my runny mucus. "You're a mess. I should kill you now and put us both out of our misery."

I blubbered some more. "I was quite happy until *you* came along."

"Type A's are never happy." He shoved his sleeve under my nose. "And look what your crying did to my coat. Black makeup everywhere! This was right out of the Goodwill bin. A genuine London Fog. You think London Fogs grow on trees?"

I was too stunned to speak and not brave enough to turn around.

"I'm going to make you *pay* for this coat." He spelled it out in my ear. "Right after I kill you, I'm going back for your bag and taking what's owing."

"I'm not paying anything for that crappy coat, dead or alive. I wouldn't even pay to have it dry-cleaned."

Not sure how much longer I could antagonize him, I slid my hand to my braid, ripped the elastic from my hair, and formed a slingshot. Then I spun around and fired it in his face.

Smack. Right in the eye!

He yelped and dropped the razor to the ground. "I knew I couldn't trust you!" He scrubbed his eye fiercely. "You *witch!*"

I'd been called worse before, but I didn't stop to point that out. Gulping for air, I stumbled away from him and swiped my bag off the ground. The helicopter was the closest thing to safety, and I ran straight for it.

Ziggy was on my heels, one hand to his eye, the other flailing in the air. I gathered every ounce of strength I had and hauled off with my bag, clouting him in the head.

He didn't seem to see that coming, which surprised me since he'd met my bag straight on once before. I only hoped the *crack* was from his skull and not my blow dryer.

For a second, his eyes glazed over and rolled up into his head. Then he collapsed knees first to the ground.

I didn't trust he'd stay down for long, and I didn't wait to find out. The aircraft was twelve feet away. I was shaking so badly my legs barely carried me there. I finally wrenched open the door, climbed into the cockpit, and fell on top of my bag onto the seat. Yee-*ouch*.

I twisted my bag out from under me, tugged the door shut, and frantically searched for a lock. *What?* No lock! How did anyone stay safe in this contraption?

I pulled on my bag straps. Maybe I could tie these around something to keep me locked in, and more importantly, keep Ziggy locked out. It had to work! I could loop them around the door handle. But what could I secure them to? *Eek!* Nothing in sight.

I felt around the door, patting my way up around the window. Wait. What was this? A metal hook? Seemed sturdy enough. I didn't know if it was a coat hanger or a place to drape curtains, and I didn't care.

I wound the straps through the handle, pressed one foot up on the door for leverage, then rose and yanked the straps up as hard as I could. If I could just stretch them...and force them over...*ackkk*! They snapped upward off the handle, and my bag sprang in my face.

I flew back and landed hard on some buttons. Before I realized what I'd done, lights flashed on the instrument panel, and the engine powered up. *Please, no!* I gawked up. And the propellers began to rotate. Yikes! Where was the horn on this thing?

Ziggy was on his feet, staggering to the helicopter. A lunatic hell-bent on a mission, oblivious to how low the propellers were spinning above him.

I screeched and punched buttons and dials, praying something I did would get him to back off. I finally remembered the throttle by the pilot's side. Not sure what this would do, I lifted the black spongy handle and rolled it left and right.

The helicopter bounced up and down on the tarmac, and Ziggy hopped back and forth like a bug about to get squashed under the landing skids.

The wind gusted around him like a small tornado, violently flipping the ends of his trench coat up in the air. Ziggy fought the wind, and in one bold move, he leaped for the door.

Bad move.

The chopper danced and dipped, and in that instant, one of the blades caught a corner of his coat and wound it around him like a cocoon, sweeping him off his feet.

In horror, I watched him spring in the air, and then *Smack*! He landed face down on top of the blade.

Aah! I leaped in my seat. I blinked and shook my head. How was this possible? Must've been my mascara running in my eyes that was playing tricks on me. Worse, it was a nightmare.

I dared look up.

Nope. Ziggy was bound to the blade, spinning above me 'round and 'round.

I had a sudden memory of a wartime video clip where a guy went through helicopter blades and survived with a broken wrist. God had taken mercy on that poor beggar. I wasn't sure Ziggy would be so fortunate.

The propellers couldn't shake him loose, and I didn't know what to do. Not having much success with the throttle, I rammed the left pedal down with my foot. The nose lurched left while the tail flew right. *Oh Lord. Forget that.* I jerked my left foot up and stabbed my right foot down, but this only caused the nose to swerve back to the right, and the tail, left.

Ziggy's body circled in and out of view, his belt flapping in the wind.

I whacked at more buttons. Something had to steady this thing! I recalled how Alan spoke into his headphones, using frequency switches. *Yes*. Maybe I'd alert the guys in the hangar. What were they doing in there anyway? Playing poker?

"Can anyone hear me?" I shouted into the headphones, pressing anything that looked like it might help.

Ziggy yelped from above.

Great. Just the person I wanted to hear from.

I finally stopped playing with the pedals and noticed the starter button. I pushed it in, and at once the engine died and the propellers wound down. Ziggy's holler faded into the distance, and suddenly I didn't see him circling above. I wasn't sure if this was good news or bad.

I yanked the fire extinguisher from above and tore out of the helicopter. If Ziggy was out there, I'd be prepared.

By now, adrenaline was speeding through my body. I was Zorro in heels, my mascara-blackened face, a mask. No one was going to touch me. I had my bag on my back and the fire extinguisher aimed clumsily like a sword. I scouted the area but didn't see Ziggy anywhere. Suddenly, I felt a tap on my shoulder.

I shrieked and wheeled around, ready to fire my weapon, but I couldn't pluck the stupid pin. Not the first time this had happened. Damn things.

The fire extinguisher was ripped from my hands, and in a fit of panic, I blinked from my empty palms up into Jock's probing face.

Terror from the entire day came to a head, and my whole body quaked in shock. Before I could gain control of myself, night closed in around me.

Chapter 15

"I know this'll be good," Jock said when I came to. "It's not everyday I see my boss fly a chopper with a raccoon mask on her face."

I sat up and blinked, confused by my surroundings.

"You're in the office." He moved closer to me on the cot and gently wiped my cheek. "We're still at the airport."

Alan offered me a glass of water. "You okay?"

"Yes. Thank you." I drank the water, swallowing some humility while I was at it for tampering with his aircraft.

He smiled with as much grace as one could expect, then left the room.

"You want to tell me what possessed you to get in that chopper and play Amelia Earhart?" Jock looked from his blackened finger into my face. "Or was the eye mask indicative of the Red Baron?"

"Don't be funny." I swung my legs past him to the floor, feeling stronger. "It was Ziggy. He was here."

"At the airport." He didn't even have the decency to ask it as a question.

"Yes!" I shot up, then back down, my legs like rubber. "He held a razor to my throat, and I got away, but only as far as the helicopter." Frustration finally hit me for being abandoned by Mr. Navy. "Where were you, by the way? You said you were paying Alan for the ride."

He nodded toward the room Alan had entered. "I was. But they were testing a new engine in the hangar, and they needed help."

I blew out air through clenched teeth. "You can't fly a helicopter, yet you can work on engines."

His voice was confident. "That about sums it up. I didn't know *you* knew how to start a chopper engine."

"I don't. I mean, I didn't. I sort of fell on top of the button."

He angled his head behind me, his gaze landing on my backside. "I see."

I knew what Jock's *I see* meant. Valentine had gotten herself into her usual trouble. Like falling into a lifeboat on a ship. Or getting locked in a laundry room—which technically wasn't my fault.

"You want me to take a look?" His tone was serious, but the gleam in his eye didn't trick me. "You may have a stellar bruise back there."

"Sure! Why don't I bend over right now!" I surprised him with *that* remark. But at the moment, sarcasm was the only thing keeping me sane.

"Look," I snapped, "Ziggy was going to kill me. I started crying, and my mascara ran down my face. I smacked him in the eye with an elastic and fled to the helicopter. I couldn't help it if the propellers flung him into outer space." I exhaled in a huff. "If anything, you should be out there looking for him, not sitting around asking questions."

"Where should I start looking? Venus or Mars?"

I couldn't blame him for the glib remark. *I* was listening to me, and I didn't make sense.

"Don't worry," he said. "We found a straight razor on the edge of the tarmac, which I reported to Romero."

"Tattletale."

He cupped my chin in his large hands, his stare powerful, brooding. By the way my heart skipped a beat, I knew nobody had dared mock him like that.

I gulped down a dry lump, waiting for him to say

something. *Darn Jock.* Trust him to get me all hot and bothered over a single word.

His gaze penetrated my eyes, his voice smooth, his words unrushed. "He'll want to pursue this and find Stoaks."

"Terrific!" I cleared my throat, ignoring his tantalizing scent and sexy aura. "That's what I want."

He gave my wrecked braid a tug. "I knew you'd be thrilled."

There was nowhere for me to hide when Romero and half the precinct sped onto the scene twenty minutes later, sirens wailing, lights flashing, tires squealing to a stop. Like they couldn't wait to see the truth behind the helicopter calamity.

The uniforms barreled out of their cruisers and joined Jock, Alan, me, and the rest of the airport crew who had flocked to the tarmac. Everyone stood there gaping at the bent chopper blades. No one had much to say. But their gazes shifted from the chopper to me and back to the chopper. Stunned was my guess. Romero was the quietest of all. I stepped a few feet back, adjusting my bag over my shoulder, avoiding his eyes at all costs.

Once everyone got over the initial shock, the cops got down to business, and once again, Jock conferred with the uniforms like it was second nature.

Aiming to look aloof and calm, I jacked up my chin and threw back my shoulders. I was Zorro in heels, right? I'd manned a helicopter—an achievement in itself. Plus, I'd almost captured an escaped convict, a murderer who had possibly murdered a second time and who was attempting it again with me! Maybe I didn't get far off the ground, and maybe I did throw Ziggy into orbit, but I refused to think of the negative. Furthermore, Ziggy shouldn't have come after me with a razor. As far as I was concerned, he got what he deserved…even if he *was* still on the loose. The scum.

Romero talked heatedly with Jock and Alan, then stalked over to me with the razor dangling from a pen, his slight limp miraculously gone. If he hadn't sworn an oath to uphold and protect, I would've dashed for my life.

"You want a turn at running this fairytale by me?" He stopped an inch from my nose, which was fighting a huge twitch.

A surge of annoyance rushed through me at his tone. Figured, he wasn't interested in asking why there were black streaks all over my face. "This was no fairytale. There was no happy ending."

He nodded, mulling this over. "My apologies. Care to explain this folktale? Myth? Fable? *Choose one.* Because I'm having a hard time believing you fired up that chopper, tangled Stoaks in the blades, and spun him in the air like a merry-go-round."

Even in the dim light reflecting off the runway, I could see the fury in his sapphire eyes—a stunning color that had lanced through me when he'd been this mad a time or ten before.

He waved his free arm in the air, his voice next to hollering. "What were you trying to do? Set a trap for Stoaks? Chase down a clue?" He exhaled loudly. "Hell, I wouldn't put it past you to try and fly that thing over a certain puppy mill."

I sprang into defensive mode, braving his piercing gaze while remaining steady on my feet. "It's all true. Except for those last three accusations," I added with a miserable pout. "And I don't *care* if you don't believe it. I wouldn't have believed it myself if I hadn't seen it with my own eyes." I brought up the scene in my mind. "At least the propellers weren't going full speed when they scooped up Ziggy."

"I'm sure he was grateful for that."

He held the razor in the air, its steel edge catching the light. "Care to tell me what *this* was doing on the tarmac?"

"It's not mine."

"No? So now you've got criminals buying beauty tools to attack others with."

I kept my voice neutral. "Better than using a gun."

"What, is that meant to make me feel better? An escaped felon threatened you with a razor, and I'm supposed to sleep like a baby tonight?"

"Will you?" I lifted my eyebrows, doubtful hope in my voice.

He dropped the razor in a plastic evidence bag an officer had quickly produced, then dragged me away from the prying eyes and ears of his men. "I've had as much today as I can take of your stubbornness."

I opened my mouth to speak but snapped it shut because of the warning look on his face.

"This morning, when I suggested a police escort back to my place, you refused. Then, you ditched Max. Even now, you should've been safe at home, either with me, or with the patrol car outside. But *no*! You'd rather be flying in helicopters over Lord-knows-where, then almost getting yourself killed."

I pinched my lips. "It wasn't over Lord-knows-where. It was over Boston."

Not pleased with my sassiness, he slid the pen in his pocket and stared into my eyes. I didn't know what he was seeing there, but he stared good and hard, not even a teensy bit distracted by the action around him. That was the thing about Romero. No matter how intense his troubles became, when he was in charge, he never let his focus wander. I gulped and searched his eyes for any signs of softening, but the lines were firm, the gaze unrelenting.

"I was sympathetic when you found Dooley's body in a beer keg," he said. "I was even understanding when I learned you went to see Luther Boyle in prison."

I gasped. "You were *not* understanding! You told me if I wasn't careful, death would come sooner than I thought."

His eyes hardened. "I would've gotten to the understanding part if you hadn't hung up on me."

He had me there.

"I also showed patience when you were accosted at Kuruc's. And you wouldn't have been accosted if you'd been safe at home instead of traipsing around Rueland like a flashing sign saying 'shoot me.'"

He held up a finger so I wouldn't interrupt. Then he glanced over at Jock thirty feet away, explaining something to a uniform. "I even kept my cool when you told me you had a date with Mr. Universe."

He glared at the helicopter and the cops examining the bent propellers, then swung his gaze back at me. "But what I can't take is knowing your stubbornness put you in extreme danger. Case in point: trying to lift that thing off the ground."

My arms were folded resolutely across my chest as I waited for an opportunity to speak.

"What I want to know is how much more trouble you're going to get into before the night's done?"

I reached over, bold as brass, and slid back the sleeve on his leather jacket. "According to Iron Man, the night's already done. So there. No more trouble to be had."

Not amused, he grabbed my wrist and banged me up against his toned abs and muscled thighs. He held on tight, not an ounce of humor in his eyes. "I'm falling hard for you, damn it, but the more I care, the crazier you become."

I wrenched away from his arms, wrestling between being turned on and feeling incensed by his words. "I am *not* crazy!"

"You're not only crazy, you're reckless and impetuous, and if you were five years old, I'd lock you in your room without your toys."

First, Ziggy called me Type A. Now this. I curled my hands into fists, my bag squashed to my side. "Good thing I'm not five years old! And if you're done harassing me, I'd like to point out I was right about Ziggy. That he attacked me here proves he was hiding in the old puppy mill. He might be there now. If you weren't so pig-headed, you'd agree."

I obviously didn't know when to shut up. "Of course, I hadn't considered the Ritz-Carlton. Maybe we should ring them up. See if Ziggy's a registered guest."

His face was stony, his stance stiff. The controlled look didn't fool me. I knew he was raging inside, and I was sure he was going to blow. "I told you we already checked out the puppy mill. Now, I'm going to say this as politely as I can." He narrowed his gaze on me and measured his words like he was speaking to a child. My heart squeezed in my chest, waiting for the inevitable.

"Stay away from that place. And. Go. Home." With that, he turned on his heel and strode over to the chopper.

Go home! Like I was a common bystander. Well, he could *go home* this! I hiked up my knee and gave him an imaginary kick in the ass.

To hell with him...*and* his fairytale insults. I whipped around, not wanting to look at Romero for another second.

Perhaps he wished to ignore my theories, but with everything I'd seen today, I wouldn't give up *or* stay away.

I peeked over my shoulder and saw the hard-ass consulting with his men. Bully for him. I paced back and forth, running what *I* knew through *my* mind.

One: Ziggy had been close. That was a fact. By all accounts, he'd killed Dooley, and he'd taunted me all day. Mode of transportation? Stolen cars. One so far. Who knew how many others he'd filched?

Two: Luther mentioning the puppy mill had weight. It would've been crazy to overlook this.

Three: I didn't know what kind of investigation Romero's men did on the place, but if I didn't accomplish anything else tomorrow, I'd go back there and survey it myself—if only for my own satisfaction.

Four: This was a race against time. I couldn't afford for Ziggy to still be on the loose once I went back to work Tuesday. I'd lose every client I had if they felt their lives were in danger. The phone was probably shrilling off the hook with cancellations at this moment.

I took a deep breath, stuffed my hands in my pockets, and trudged over to Jock's bike. I stole one last look at the helicopter, cringing at the bent blades. I'd come close to making an accidental capture, but good fortune had not been on my side.

Don't dwell on the past, Valentine. Tomorrow would be different.

I was still thinking about this when Jock deposited me on my doorstep at 1:00 a.m. An end to a blessed day.

"Romero didn't look too happy being dragged out to the airport tonight," he said, making matters worse. "Just how many homicides *have* you been involved in?" This was asked with a mix of respect and incredulity.

"You already know the answer to that." I unlocked the door and flicked on the light. "And don't talk to me about Romero. I've had enough of his dirty glares and heated temper for one day."

Jock's frame filled the doorway, arms crossed, face frowning. "Yeah. Can't imagine why he didn't understand your decision to start a chopper and bounce it around the tarmac."

I caught him grinning. "You think that's funny?" I shoved him out the door. "Laugh at *this!*" I slammed the door in his face, turned the deadbolt, and slid the chain across. "Ha!" I hoped my voice traveled through the door.

I waited a beat until I heard Jock's bike thunder away. Good. *Wiseass.* Making fun of me and my efforts.

I stamped into the bathroom, switched on the light, and screamed at my reflection in the mirror.

"To hell with men," I declared, washing myself clean. "Try to defend yourself, and where does it get you?"

Yitts rolled around on her back, playing with her catnip ball, not too interested in listening to me argue with myself.

My cleanser tumbled to the floor with a clatter, startling Yitts to her feet. She hissed and arched her back, ready for a fight. Once she realized the sky wasn't falling, she settled on her haunches, snorting relief out her nose.

I gave my own snort, picturing Romero's threatening look tonight. I brushed my teeth, mumbling the whole time my mouth was frothing with toothpaste about how unfair he'd been.

That was fine. I didn't need him or his smart attitude. He could carry on with his investigation. Tomorrow, I'd carry on with mine.

Chapter 16

It was early the next morning when I woke up, possibly because I hadn't slept well the night before.

My body felt bruised, my head sore. And my face was probably going to break out from all the mascara that had saturated my pores.

I rolled out of bed, not feeling especially proud of the way I'd talked to Romero last night. But dang, he could be an ignoramus. And *bullheaded*. A macho, Italian, bullheaded ignoramus. With swarthy looks, a hot body, gorgeous eyes...

My cheeks flushed, and a burning pulse throbbed below. Darn it! Being mad at Romero was turning me on.

I fanned myself and centered on what I needed to do today. Forget Mr. Detective. He could search the Ritz-Carlton for Ziggy. I had other plans.

First thing I needed to do was talk to Mrs. Calvino's son Dom at Lumber Mart. In the grand scheme of things, I was certain Ziggy had delivered the dildo yesterday morning, but maybe Dom had seen something when he'd arrived at his mom's. Something that had stood out. Something I hadn't noticed.

I summoned images from last night's tour over the puppy mill. Since Ziggy had attacked me so close to the building, he'd basically tipped his hand that this was his hiding place. He probably wasn't there now because he'd figure the cops would look for him there first. Ha! Forget about the cops. Maybe Dom had not only observed something from his mom's driveway, but maybe he could provide another clue on where to look for Ziggy.

What's more, I still needed proof that Ziggy killed Dooley. I wanted justice for Dooley, and if Ziggy was his murderer, he needed to pay for his crime. As it stood now, the puppy mill was the best place to look for that proof.

Since the hospital was only a few miles from Lumber Mart, I'd stop there after for my weekly visit with the kids. Let them turn me into the Bride of Frankenstein. This case was getting under my skin, and I reasoned that an hour's reprieve wouldn't hurt anything. Which reminded me...I needed to drop by the shop and replenish my bag with nail stickers. The kids loved peeling those suckers off the sheet and planting them all over me.

A smile erupted on my face. If I made one child burst into giggles from my wacky appearance, it was worth the trouble.

I had to pick up Max, too, but he'd be making pizza dough until noon. That suited me fine. I'd either take him home or see if he wanted to accompany me back to the puppy mill. I wouldn't pressure him either way. His friend Freddie had been murdered by the hands of two goons, and staking out the puppy mill might bring back the pain of losing his pal.

Yitts meowed in no uncertain terms that she was hungry and needed her brushing. I nuzzled her under my chin, then set her down and brushed her black fur until it gleamed.

"Wherever Ziggy is today," I told her, "he won't be bothering me anymore. After being tossed from the propellers last night, he'll be lucky to be alive." Which also gave me the confidence to visit the sick kids. If Ziggy wasn't dead, he'd be laying low.

Yitts took her paw and tapped my hand. I stared down at her, realizing I'd stopped brushing. "Tyrant," I said, picking up the pace.

By the time I'd fed Yitts and gotten myself together, it was twenty to nine. Instead of making up for yesterday's hair disaster and doing something stunning with my locks, I twisted them into a simple bun. Lumber Mart's doors were probably already open. I wanted to be there with my questions ready.

I gave myself a final shot of Musk, then put out the garbage and took a good look around the neighborhood. Gray skies…again, accompanied with heavy clouds. There were a few stragglers on their way to school. No predators stalking the street.

Ray Donoochi backed out of his driveway and gave me a toot. Always good to know an officer was on duty.

A shiver rushed through me, and I knew temperatures would struggle to rise. I went back in the house, wrapped my long red scarf around my neck four times, and grabbed my bag. I warmed up the car, cruised down Orchard to Wellington, took the roundabout to Hemlock, and pulled into Lumber Mart as my car clock read nine.

Dom Calvino wore a nametag shaped like a happy beaver and was behind the counter at the back of the store, helping a customer. Dom was pushing forty and had the same shock of gray hair that fell in a wavy swoop over his forehead like his mother's.

He looked up at me, gave a quick nod, and said he'd be a few minutes. No problem, I said. I'd look around till he was free since I loved lumber stores. White lie. The smell of pine took me back to shop class in high school—not a good memory—and looking at floor tiles and paint samples made my eyes glaze over.

His customer left with his own glazed look when Dom handed him a two-page invoice and told him to meet the forklifts out back.

Stretching my scarf down from my neck, I moseyed up to the counter and introduced myself to Dom. Not surprisingly, he knew who I was. The chuckle that escaped his mouth was a dead giveaway.

I asked if he'd seen anything suspicious yesterday morning when he arrived at his mom's.

"You mean did I see any more deliveries? Like a Turbo Wand Massager? Passion plugs?" He leaned in. "Or a supersized stallion suction-cup dildo? Whew." He rolled his eyes. "Hang that baby in the barn and see how limber you are."

"What?" I backed away, eewing inside. "*No*. I only had one delivery. I wondered if you saw anything else in the neighborhood. Something peculiar or out of place."

He tucked a paper in a folder and stared past me into the distance. After a few seconds, I waved my hand in front of his face. "Dom?"

He blinked, his stare drawn back to me. "*Yeah*, there *was* something that seemed odd. I was getting the air purifier out of my trunk when this white car drove down the street."

"A white car."

"Yes."

"What's so odd about a white car?"

His lips flattened. "Nothing per se, but this one had a logo on the door, like a plumber or an electrician's logo."

I ruminated on this. "A car? Not a van or truck?"

"Definitely a car." He shrugged. "I *told* you something seemed odd."

I frowned. "Maybe it was a company car, or someone was paying somebody a visit." It'd been kind of early for that, and I couldn't think of anyone on the street who drove a company car with a logo on it. Ray Donoochi occasionally brought a cruiser home during the day, but a black-and-white with lights on top was easily recognizable.

"Could be. But the woman driving the car slowed down and seemed to take a good look at your place."

The hairs on the back of my neck stood at attention. "Woman?"

"Yeah. I couldn't see much from where I was standing, and it wasn't that light yet, but I'm sure it was a woman."

"Was she blond? Dark? Redheaded?"

"Like I said, it wasn't that light out. Sorry. Wish I could be more help."

I thanked Dom and left Lumber Mart a little shaky in my boots. Who was this woman? And why was she interested in my place? Did she know something about the dildo delivery? Did she know Ziggy? I racked my brain for missing pieces to the mystery but couldn't think of what I'd overlooked.

Hang on a minute. The female voice on the phone, the one that had upset Dooley. Of course! I hadn't stopped to think about that in a while. Was the woman in the white car the one who'd called the restaurant? But who was she? And what was her connection to Dooley's death, and Ziggy...and me?

Jimmy had said there were no women in Dooley's life. And Ziggy had been in prison. Not exactly prime real estate for carrying on a torrid love affair. Where did that leave me?

I stuffed myself back in my Bug, shook off the jitters, and put the car in gear. I had things to do, and I didn't have time to waste.

Ten minutes later, I swung into the parking at the back of the shop and pulled up beside Phyllis's rusty whale of a car.

What was Phyllis doing here on a Monday when we were closed?

I unlocked the back door and trotted to the front of the salon, the sound of a humming hair dryer greeting me, the usual chemical odors filling my nose. I rounded the corner from the hall and saw the croaky-voiced kid from Friar Tuck's under the dryer.

He was in his tunic and medieval boots, towel around his shoulders, felt crown by his side. A small flask of booze was perched between his thighs, and he was singing merrily to himself, drumming his head against the inside of the dryer hood.

There was hair on the floor by Phyllis's station, which sat unswept. Naturally. If Phyllis had just done a haircut, she wouldn't be in a hurry to clean up the clippings. Instead, she sat amid the mess in her hydraulic chair across from Friar Tuck. She was wearing her white smock, and she was flipping through one of the new magazines I'd restocked yesterday.

I rapped my knuckles on the wall, mildly irritated. "Phyllis?"

She jerked upright in her chair. "Huh?"

"What are you doing here?" I flung my bag on the dryer chair beside the kid. "And what's Friar Tuck doing under the dryer, drinking booze? It's not even noon yet. Plus, I don't think he's even of age."

Phyllis's eyes shifted from the quarter-empty flask, to me, with an uh-oh look on her face. "I had one last tint job to squeeze in before graduating from my course. Austin agreed to help me out." She sounded so proud. "After all, I buy enough day-old donuts to keep Friar Tuck's in business."

I couldn't refute that. "I thought you were having your first class on tinting yesterday."

"It's a fast-moving course."

Evidently.

I tilted my head at Austin and noticed blue gunk on his brows and lashes. Plastic wrap covered the gunk and spiraled around his head like a blindfold. He didn't appear bothered. Along with singing and drumming his head against the dryer hood, he was playing an air guitar, making funny burping sounds. "That still doesn't explain why he seems half tanked."

Phyllis puckered her lips. "He said he wasn't making any commission on my day-old donuts, and if I wanted him as a *happy*, willing model, I'd have to buy him a bottle of rum."

I sighed. "Did it occur to you that he asked you to purchase a bottle of rum because he *couldn't*? Because he's under age?"

Her eyebrows slid up. "No. But drinking it did wonders for his jumpiness. He was squirming and squealing like a pig when I put bleach on his eyelashes. And look at him now. Happy as a clam."

My breathing hitched in my throat. "Phyllis, you put bleach on his *eyelashes*?"

She wriggled off her chair. "The last assignment said to do something unique."

I couldn't even think of the outcome to this. I threw up my hands and headed into the dispensary.

The timer went off with a ding, and Austin kicked his leg in the air, strumming a riff, singing the lyrics to "We Are the Champions." Happy as a clam.

Phyllis strolled to the front and dropped her magazine on a pile with the other new ones, not in much of a hurry to tend to her client. Didn't matter anyway. Austin blindly took a swig of his rum, screwed the cap back on, and continued singing he was the champion.

I slammed drawers, hunting for my stack of nail stickers, only coming up with three sheets. Strange. I had dozens last time I'd checked.

I marched over to the manicure table and searched there. Zilch. I poked my head up at Phyllis across the room. "Do you know where all my nail stickers are?"

She led Austin over to the sink. "Yeah, I took a bunch home."

"What for?"

"You're not going to believe this."

Would anything Phyllis did ever come as a surprise? "Try me."

She leaned Austin back in his chair, shrugging at me. "I was having blueberries for dessert one night and thought I'd make a shake. Ends up the lid wasn't on the blender right, and I sort of had a blueberry explosion."

Austin hiccupped. "Cooool."

"Sooo?" I was standing at the foot of her station, waiting for the good part.

"So, I couldn't get the blueberry stains off the walls, and I thought why not cover the blue spots with nail stickers."

"Why not? I'll tell you why not." I was doing my best to control my anger, but I had to loosen my scarf around my neck because I was boiling inside. "Nail stickers are for *nails*. The only other reason I order these decals is to let the hospital kids have their fun with them."

"*Pff.*" She waved a wet hand in the air. "They'll get over it. You can always pick up cheap stickers at the dollar store."

My jaw dropped at her lack of compassion. "They like nail stickers because they're more intricate, and they revolve around beauty, and—" Why was I explaining anything to her?

"*Aaaaah!*" Austin pressed his nose to the mirror, scrubbing his forehead.

Phyllis and I had been so busy arguing we hadn't paid attention to him slinking out of his chair.

"Stop screaming!" Phyllis barely gave Austin a second glance. "You sound like a girl."

Everything screeched to a halt around me, those words penetrating my skull. *Austin sounded like a girl.* That was it. A woman's voice inside a man. That was what kept nagging me about Ziggy. His tone was unnatural, soft, feminine, whereas during the perm-rod incident years ago his voice had been deep, manly. Yow! Was it true that if a man lost his pride—so to speak—his voice climbed a few octaves?

The jokes about Ziggy becoming a soprano had been constant, but until now, I hadn't stopped to consider the soprano phenomenon could be true.

My thoughts were jumping leaps and bounds, coming back again to the woman caller. Was it possible Ziggy was the one who'd made those disturbing calls to Dooley at the restaurant? Threatening or telling Dooley he wanted to speak to him in person? Maybe Dooley agreed, thinking they'd clear up any misunderstanding, talking face to face.

There had to be a record of calls from prison, and it was a lead I could share with Romero. Unless Detective Smartass had already investigated this. But it all made sense and would've explained Dooley letting Ziggy into the Wee Irish Dude. Only thing was, if the feminine voice belonged to Ziggy, who was the woman in the white car? Was she even significant?

Austin shrieked again, dragging my thoughts back to the present.

With clean-cut hair, average weight, and a pimply face, Austin was a typical-looking youth…except for his pale white lashes and brows that were coming off in clumps. On top of that, the bleach must've seeped into his hair when he was knocking his head on the dryer, because the front half had turned white.

He flicked mushy bits of hair from his fingers, blinking at his reflection. "I look like Colonel Sanders." His bottom lip quivered, his eyes wide. "Except *he* had fried chicken. All I've got is six eyelashes. Count 'em. *Six!* What's my mom going to say?"

"Stop whining," Phyllis said. "You still look better than the last guy who came in here."

Austin took a gulp of rum, and I swiveled my head to Phyllis. "Last guy?" I glanced down at the clippings on the floor, assuming they'd belonged to Austin, pre-bleach. But now that I studied them, I realized they were a different shade of hair. "What last guy?"

"The guy who was waiting at the door when I got here this morning. Scrapes on his face, arm in a homemade sling. Said he had a funeral to go to and he needed a haircut, but all the salons were closed." Phyllis scratched her head, grimacing. "He looked so beat up, I thought he was talking about his own funeral."

I swallowed back a tremor working its way up my spine. "Was this guy wearing a beige trench coat? Maybe a London Fog?"

"How did you know?" Her mouth hung open like she was talking to a bona fide psychic. "Though I wouldn't say it was much of a coat. Sort of tattered, like he got it out of the Goodwill bin. And one sleeve was all black. Must've been grease or something."

Oy. Arm in a sling. Scrapes on his face. Soiled frayed coat.

"Phyllis, that was Ziggy Stoaks you let into the salon."

"Who's Ziggy Stoaks?"

I cringed, not surprised I had to spoon-feed her news in small doses. "The guy I helped put away for murdering Max's friend. He escaped from prison the other day. We think he killed Dooley. Now he's trying to kill me."

"The perm-rod guy?"

"Yes."

"And I just cut his hair?"

"*Yes.*"

She stood motionless for a second, letting this sift through her brain. Then she took three large strides over to Austin, ripped the flask from his hand, and took a slug of rum. Her eyes got watery, and she clutched her throat.

Phyllis wasn't much of a drinker. In fact, I couldn't remember ever seeing her down straight liquor. Coughing and sputtering, she dodged for the hose, yanked up the tap, and guzzled cold water. "How was I supposed to know I was cutting a murderer's hair?" she gasped, slamming down the tap. "He said he knew you. I figured I was doing the right thing."

Phyllis never did the right thing. One time that would've been in her favor, she chose to play the humanitarian.

"He wasn't even grateful…the scumbag." She wiped her mouth and threw a hand on her hip. "Would you believe he complained about his haircut? Said one side was bushier than the other. Lowlife. What nerve."

"Yeah. Imagine that." A murderer with standards.

But it was unsettling. After ornamenting the front window yesterday with his repugnant drawing, then trying to shoot me at Kuruc's and abduct me from the airport, why had Ziggy risked visiting the shop again? To put another scare in me? To show he wasn't giving up, even if he was injured? The churning in my stomach told me he was still lurking about, ready to pounce again.

"And when he said he knew me, you didn't question how?"

Phyllis shook her head. "I figured he was an old boyfriend or something."

"Thanks." Couldn't blame her there. It was no secret I'd dated louts before. Maybe not murderers or animal abusers, but jerks all the same.

Perhaps Ziggy thought he was being clever, revisiting the shop, leaving his scent like a dog. Well, I was done with his games. Done with being taunted. Done waiting for him to hunt me down and strike again. There had to be clues to this whole mystery at the puppy mill, and I'd find them. I wasn't about to quit now.

"Uh, can I go now?" Austin piped, felt crown in hand, a pleading look on his face. To his credit, he had sobered up quickly.

Phyllis tossed him the flask, tugged her phone from her smock pocket, and told him to smile.

"*Smile.*" He squawked. "What have I got to smile about?"

"For helping me graduate from this course. I've fulfilled all the criteria and completed my work on the minimum number of models."

Austin gaped from Phyllis to me like he couldn't believe his ears. "You mean you did this on someone else?" He took a moment to absorb this. "And he's still living?"

Phyllis fiddled with her camera. "Not only is he living, but he *liked* his new look. Now *smile.*"

Austin worked up a smile, but he looked more constipated than anything.

Satisfied with her shot, Phyllis slid her phone in her pocket. She pinched a brown eyebrow pencil from the makeup tray and drew two lines on Austin's forehead.

"There." She plunked the pencil in his palm. "Wear this until your eyebrows grow back. Your mother will never ask questions."

Austin stared from the pencil back up at Phyllis. "How long will that be?"

"Four months, tops."

He gawked at himself in the mirror. "What about my hair? It's *white*."

Phyllis rolled her eyes like she was dealing with a halfwit. "Don't you know anything? White hair on men is distinguished. You'll have all the girls chasing you down the street."

"I don't want all the girls chasing me," he croaked. "I need to clear up my acne first."

"Then you should lay off the fried donuts you make next door. They're nothing but sugar, empty calories, and bad for your health. Eventually, it'll all go to your hips."

Straight from the horse's mouth.

Austin let out a high-pitched whimper, hung his head, and traipsed out the back door.

Annoyed that I was even considering phoning Romero after the way he'd hollered at me last night, I swallowed my pride and called his cell number. It went straight to voicemail, so I left a short message about checking prison records to see if Ziggy had made calls from there to the Wee Irish Dude.

I didn't see the point in telling Romero about Ziggy's latest visit to the salon. We knew who we were looking for, and it wouldn't change anything. Either way, we still needed to find Ziggy. This only confirmed the best way to catch him was to look for evidence at the puppy mill.

I'd wanted to pop in at the hospital today, but I decided to postpone my visit. The fact that Ziggy was still walking on two legs made me apprehensive to go anywhere near Rueland Memorial. Bad enough he was attempting to kill me. I couldn't subject the sick kids to possible danger.

I left Phyllis to clean up her mess, then motored to

Jimmy's. It was ten after eleven. Surely, they'd be wrapping up their pizza-dough-making party by now.

"What's with the Bruins jersey?" I asked Max when he opened Jimmy's front door.

He held out the *B*-embossed black-and-gold jersey from the hem. "Being I slept in my clothes, Jimmy offered me clean duds. It was either this or a surfing T-shirt. And I thought it was a bit chilly to be sporting beach clothes."

"Good point."

I walked through the doorway and looked around. "Where is Jimmy?"

"Went back to the restaurant. Said he had to face it sooner or later."

We lowered our eyes at this. The next few weeks wouldn't be easy for Jimmy. How would he manage the restaurant without Dooley? Who would be his head chef?

"Look!" Max ran into the kitchen and came back holding a big plastic bowl of dough.

I scrunched up my nose. "I'm looking."

"That all you can say?" He shoved the bowl under my nose. "Smell it. You love the aroma of fresh-made dough. Isn't it heavenly?"

I inhaled deeply. "Yes. It'd probably be *more* heavenly coming out of a brick oven with pizza fixings on top."

He sniffed, nose high. "No need to get persnickety. As soon as I get home, I'm going to add the toppings. You'll see. This will be the best pizza in the world!"

I rolled my eyes at his exaggeration and followed him into the kitchen.

"You want to come over and help?" He spun around, excitement dancing in his eyes. "We'll have a pizza party."

I thought of Ziggy and the puppy mill, and what lay ahead. Not that a pizza party didn't sound fabulous, but I wouldn't be able to relax knowing there was a killer loose. A killer who wanted me dead.

"Another time," I said. "Right now, I've got things to do."

"Such as?" He plopped the bowl on the kitchen counter. "Wait a minute. You haven't said a word about last night." He thrust his nose an inch from my face, looking for telltale signs of my night with Jock.

It seemed like a week had passed since I'd last spoken to Max. I hadn't told him about my harrowing experience at Kuruc's or Ziggy's second attack at the airport. I took a deep breath, pushed him back from almost crushing my toes, and filled him in on everything.

His eyes bugged out like I'd announced Dolce & Gabbana went bankrupt. "You flew a *helicopter*?"

Max couldn't just listen to a story from beginning to end like most normal people. He had to interrupt and echo the bizarre bits.

I took my fingers and slapped his jaw tight. "That's not what I said."

"I heard what you said. You got a helicopter off the ground."

"That doesn't mean I flew it anywhere. Pay attention!"

"I *am* paying attention! I still haven't heard what happened with Jock while you were flying all over Boston." He studied my face, peering from my one eye to the other. "Did he jump your bones? Are you part of the mile-high club?"

"No, and no." I lugged out my phone. "But I did take shots of the view."

"Shots of the *view*! What's so great about that?"

"Nothing! Do you want to see them or not?"

He gestured his hand at me like *let me have it.*

I gave him a galled look. Why did I put up with his lunacy? I scrolled through my photos and showed him the best pictures that didn't have my finger or the helicopter window frame in the way.

He took control of the phone, angling it this way and that. "You're getting better at this. I can almost tell that's the John Hancock building."

"Smart aleck." I seized the phone back. "You're lucky I took any pictures at all." I scrolled to the last shot, realizing I hadn't looked at it yet.

Max leaned in, watching me enlarge it. "What's that? What are you looking at?"

"Precisely what I was trying to share with you before you went on a tangent about Jock." I turned the phone toward him. "This is the puppy mill where Ziggy and Luther ran their business."

I shuddered, thinking again about their vicious deeds, then forgot about myself and peeked at Max, who seemed to be taking this okay. "It's right beside the airport. *That's* where Ziggy was hiding." I said this like I was chief commander of the case. "Luther basically handed us the information on a tray."

He thought for a moment. "I don't remember Luther handing us anything on a tray."

"Maybe I'm better at reading between the lines." I couldn't help but give a smug nod.

"If you were so good at reading between the lines, sugar, you'd know that our Herculean friend didn't take you on a tour of Boston for the good of your health. And if you weren't so against dating an employee, you'd see exactly what this hunk has to offer."

He looked me square in the eye, his voice laced with sarcasm. "Maybe I'm better at reading between the lines than you think."

I bristled when Max got self-righteous with me. "Can we get back to the case? I have more important things to think about than Jock's libido."

I suppressed the urge to fan myself, because deep down I knew Max was right. Jock had shown all the romantic signs on our tour of Boston. Checking my seatbelt as a façade for brushing his fingers across my breasts. Snuggling close to me in our seats. Taking my hand in his and massaging his thumb seductively across my skin. Most of all, what caught my breath was the way he'd gazed into my eyes and said he wouldn't force me to do anything I wasn't comfortable with. On the surface, he was talking about taking the helicopter ride, but we both knew he meant more. Much more.

"Okay," Max mused. "You think the old puppy mill was Ziggy's home base."

"Without question."

"Is that what Romero believes?"

I tensed. "Romero's probably scouting the halls of the Ritz-Carlton."

"I take that as a no." Max grabbed the phone again and zoomed in some more. "What you're saying could make sense since Ziggy came at you on the airstrip with a razor. And the airstrip is next to the woods that surround the puppy mill."

Finally. Someone who saw it my way. "*Thank* you. That's what I tried to tell everyone. Plus, there's got to be proof there that he killed Dooley."

Max looked from me back to the phone. "Hey…what's this?"

"What?" I scooched closer to him, our cheeks pressed together.

"*This.*" He pointed to a dark patch on the roof. "Looks like a trap door. If the place was boarded up, maybe this was how Ziggy was sneaking in."

"From the roof?" When he put his mind to it, Max could be Sherlock Holmes.

"Why not?"

"I guess it's possible." I thought this through. "No matter how he gained entrance into the place, the roof could be *our* way of gaining entrance. All we'd need is a ladder…and not being spotted by overhead planes."

Max made a face. "Rueland Area Airport isn't exactly Logan International. How often do you suppose planes…or helicopters," he added mischievously, "are flying in and out?"

"Agreed. It's not a busy airport."

I took the phone from Max. "Shall we go see? If I'm right, and Ziggy's decamped from the puppy mill, we're not putting ourselves in any danger by going there."

Max packed up the bread machine, snatched the bowl of dough, and headed for the door.

"Wait!" I dumped the phone in my bag and sped up to him. "You sure you want to do this?"

He didn't stop to think. "Sure as I've ever been." A trace of sorrow crept into his voice. "I still miss Freddie, and I'll always be grateful that last time you caught his killers on your own. But this is unfinished business, baby. It's time I had a shot at this." He took a step for the door, then paused and turned back. "And let's not forget... Jimmy's my friend, too."

I liked his self-confidence. "Okay. Let's go."

Chapter 17

We darted into Jimmy's garage, nabbed his ladder and an old blanket I found by the workbench, wrapped the blanket around the ladder, and tied it to the roof of Daisy Bug. We didn't assume for a minute that there'd be a ladder at the puppy mill, and there was no harm in borrowing the Skink's. The note I'd left in the ladder's place explained our actions along with a promise we'd return it in good shape. Wasn't *I* the positive thinker!

Because the ladder was extra long, I undid my red scarf from my neck and braided it around the part sticking out over the back of the car, tying the ends into a pretty bow.

Max finished loading his stuff in the backseat, then straightened and gave me his deadpan face. "Do you have to fancy up everything?"

I looked at my handiwork and smiled. "What do *you* think?"

"I think it's a disease."

I stuck out my tongue in fun, and we hopped in our seats and drove off with the scarf's bow flapping in the wind.

Within minutes, I curved into the long driveway leading to the puppy mill and crawled to a stop under a canopy of tall pine trees near the low, one-story building.

We solemnly looked from the deserted structure to the small, corroded cages strewn across the property, neither one of us too eager to make the next move.

"Now what?" Max ventured, repeating the same question he'd asked twenty-four hours ago when we'd arrived at the jail in Norfolt.

I swallowed down the lump forcing its way up my throat. "We take the ladder and climb it to the roof."

"Uh, correction," he said. "*You* take the ladder and climb it to the roof." He glanced down at his clothes. "I don't want to ruin Jimmy's jersey."

"How selfless of you." I yanked up my jacket zipper and clutched my bag. "Fine. *I'll* climb it."

"Thanks for offering." He gave me an impish smile, and we hauled ourselves out of the car. "Of course, if Romero were here instead of at the Ritz-Carlton, he could be doing this himself." He swung the car door shut. "But since he's not, I'll scout the area on ground."

We waited until a helicopter flew by, then we unhitched the ladder, carried it to the building, and propped it against the wall. I freed my scarf and wrapped it around my neck while I surveyed the windows and doors of the puppy mill. Everything was securely boarded up, and an old strip of crime scene tape dangled from the door. No sense starting there.

Max, on the other hand, was tugging on the doorknob as if he'd cried "*open sesame!*" and been cheated entry.

"*Max!*" I whispered hoarsely from the ladder. "What are you doing?"

"What does it look like?"

"It looks like you're trying to get into a locked building."

He stopped wrenching on the door. "If you knew the answer to the question, why'd you ask?"

Oh Lord, give me strength. "I told you the place was boarded up. Now go inspect the area. Look for anything that might be used as evidence against Ziggy in Dooley's murder. If I find the trap door is open, I'll let you know."

"Ten-four." He trudged to the woods.

I hooked my bag over my back, gathered my nerves, and mounted the rungs of the ladder. I didn't know if Max had stopped to realize we were technically breaking and entering, and if Romero found out, he'd throw the book at us. I, for one, wasn't going to bring this up.

I was about to heave myself up onto the roof when a small plane unexpectedly roared overhead. I ducked. First a helicopter. Then a plane. It was all quiet on the western front until we showed up. Now all of a sudden, it was rush hour in Boston.

Focusing on the job at hand, I swung my leg onto the roof and pulled myself up. I dusted myself off and tiptoed over to the trap door. At least, it resembled a trap door in the photo. I knelt in front of it and tried to wiggle it loose. To no avail. There were no hinges and no handle. In point of fact, it wasn't a door at all. It was simply a patched piece of metal bolted down to the roof. *Damn.*

I let out a sigh and looked around. Nothing else up here that would allow access into the building. I shimmied back down the ladder and was one foot from the ground when I sensed movement behind me. The air was still, but there was no mistaking the sounds of twigs snapping and dead leaves rustling.

I gulped, frozen in place, telling myself it was only a squirrel looking for food. Or a bird. Or Max. But the dread pelting my spine told me it was none of these.

"One more step, sweetheart, and you're down." The high-pitched voice was persuasive, commanding. "Come on. You can do it. Then turn around real slow."

I could barely move for the terror gripping me. Like a stick soldier, I clomped the last step off the ladder and tapped my foot on the ground.

"There you go," the voice said. "Now turn around."

Panic choked me from the inside out, and my heart was racing with fear. I slowly pivoted around and faced Ziggy ten feet away in his tattered London Fog, a haphazard sling around one arm, a gun aimed at my head with the other.

This was the first time I'd heard Ziggy speak in a normal tone. No whispering. No frenzied yelling. Plus, no fierce winds, plane engines, or other rackets interfering with his words. Ziggy was definitely a soprano. But why was he still here?

"We're not going to have any accidents," he said. "That means no helicopter rides, no snapping elastics, and nix the lethal perm rods. I'll say what I need to say. Then I'm going to kill you." He glanced from his gun back to me. "Got that?"

I swallowed dryly and nodded.

"Good. Now put your bag down."

I slid my bag to my feet. My eyes never left his face, or his hair and the butcher job Phyllis had given him.

He narrowed his gaze on me, stepping a foot closer. "What's got you so entranced?"

I tightened my lips, holding my tongue, but his lopsided haircut and high voice was unraveling me. "Nothing?"

"No…no. It's something all right." Instinctively, he patted his head. "I know what you're gawking at. It's my freakin' haircut."

"Okay." I shrugged, astonishment taking over the fear. "It's a little…off-center."

"*Off-center!* It looks like I've been prepped for a lobotomy. That dumb broad who works for you even snipped my ear." He bent the top of his ear down with the tip of his gun and showed me a bandage stuck on top. "I should've shot her when I had the chance."

"It's your own fault." I stuck out my chest, not sure where the sudden bravery had come from. "What were you doing at the shop, anyway?"

"I needed a haircut and thought why not visit my favorite stylist."

His compliment didn't flatter me.

"Would've been the perfect opportunity to kill you, too, but when I found that dumb broad there instead, I decided why not? I wanted to spruce up my look anyway before I skipped town and started a new life."

He shook his head in disgust. "But I can tell you, you've lost a customer. How can you employ such a failure? You should take a course on how to run a successful business."

This wasn't the first time someone had questioned my business acumen. But I wasn't in the mood for a lecture.

"Why are you doing this, Ziggy? The police know you killed Dooley. And they know I'm here. You might as well give up."

"Ha! You're a dirty little liar. I heard you and Pretty Boy talking before. I know that boyfriend of yours ain't anywhere near here."

Darn! Why hadn't I been more careful? If I'd had any sense, I wouldn't have tried to play the hero without some sort of backup. I instantly recalled my heated debate with Romero at the airport last night. Right. I was as good as being on my own. And Max was likely out in the back forty, scouting for mushrooms for his pizza.

"You're not bringing me in again," Ziggy hissed. "That clear? I'm going to ruin your life like you ruined mine."

I didn't know what he had in store for me, but my throat constricted, and my head spun from the thought of him disfiguring and torturing me. I'd escaped death last night by the grace of God. I wasn't deluding myself into thinking I'd be granted any favors today.

We stared mutely at each other for an intense moment, and out of nowhere a tear rolled down my cheek, making room for another.

"Don't give me any of that crying nonsense." He shook his gun unsteadily in my direction. "Last time you tried that, I got an elastic in the eye. Plus, you ruined your makeup and stained my coat." He swung his sooty sleeve in the air as proof. "I can put up with a lot of things, but looking at you with a black roadmap on your face is more than any human can handle."

"I wouldn't give you the satisfaction of crying!" I swiped away the tears in anger and said a prayer for strength and protection.

My legs wobbled under me, and my stomach muscles

tensed. I cast a look where I'd last seen Max disappear, hoping he'd have my back. Nothing. No movement. No Max. Forget the mushrooms. He was probably already home, playing Emeril Lagasse…or Rachael Ray.

Ziggy moved closer, his face unyielding. "As far as Dooley goes, he had it coming—the chicken. If he'd taken care of you like I'd asked, he'd still be here."

I felt a surge of sorrow for Dooley, dying nobly on my behalf. And since dying was at the forefront of my mind, I stared at the barrel of Ziggy's gun, terrified his shaky grip would falter and he'd fire the thing prematurely.

I took another breath for courage, guessing my next remark wouldn't gain me any brownie points. "Sure, he'd still be here—all set to go back to prison. I mean, what kind of moron asks a recently released convict to commit murder?" I was taking liberties left and right, but as long as I kept him talking, I had a chance to get myself out of this mess.

He spit on the ground by my feet. "A moron with a vision, that's who. Dooley was free. I wasn't. Telling him you were my girlfriend was a ploy to get him to hunt you down. We were buddies in prison. I thought he'd follow through. But I should've known better. You want anything done right in this world, you gotta do it yourself."

Who would've thought Ziggy had such a strong work ethic?

"But to set the record straight, I didn't kill Dooley. I would've, but someone got to him first."

What? My mouth went dry at this bombshell, and for a second it seemed like my heart stopped beating. If Ziggy wasn't Dooley's murderer, then who was? I swallowed back in shock, and before I had a chance to speak, he gestured to the building.

"By the way," he said, smirking, "good try, looking for an entrance to the puppy mill. Truth is, I never hid inside. Luther and I had made a survivalist shelter underground stocked with food and provisions in case we ever needed to lay low." He motioned over his shoulder. "The trap door entrance was so well camouflaged, it obviously went unnoticed when the mill was closed and yesterday when the local yokels came looking for me."

He chuckled. "Poor buggers. Probably still scratching their heads, wondering where I've gone."

His evil stare moved from me to his gun. "They can search all they want. I have *this* for protection. Thank you, Two-Notes."

I was still taking this all in, but I gulped at the mention of Candace's grandpa's name. "Two-Notes?"

He grinned. "Yeah. The old geezer arranged it for me. He still has connections to the outside." He gave a slight nod. "Don't let his appearance fool you. He's in the slammer for a reason."

I gave this a brief thought, my mind moving to Ziggy's time in prison, then his escape, and finally the delivery to my door.

"Did Two-Notes also provide you with the dildo you left on my porch?"

He scrunched up his nose. "Huh?"

"You heard me. You delivered a dildo with a perm rod wrapped around it early yesterday morning."

"Lady, where are you getting this stuff?"

My mouth felt like sandpaper. "You mean you *didn't* deliver the dildo?"

"No, I did not." He lifted his chin, insulted I would suggest such a thing. "Sure, I fancied up your salon window, but I wouldn't touch one of those apparatuses with a ten-foot pole."

The look in his eyes told me he wasn't joking, and I believed him. Just because he'd been in jail for murder didn't mean he was kinky. If Ziggy didn't deliver the dildo—or kill Dooley—then who did?

I was back to the beginning of this nightmare, speculating who was responsible for scaring me senseless with this sick joke, when without warning, Ziggy tossed his gun to the forest floor.

"Hell, I don't need a weapon. I'm going to enjoy killing you with my bare hands."

He jumped and slammed me to the ground, wrapping my scarf around his knuckles. "This is for making me a bloody alto." He tightened the scarf around my neck.

I squawked in fright. "You mean a *soprano*." If I was going to die, I might as well die in the right.

He bared his teeth and pounded my head up and down until my hair flew out of its knot. "And this is for putting Luther and me behind bars."

The air was getting sucked out of me, and I was afraid I was going to lose consciousness. He lifted me a foot off the ground by my jacket lapels and hammered me back down. A sharp sting struck me between the shoulders, and I moaned.

Ziggy barked in laughter, secure in the knowledge that this time he wasn't going to lose.

We rolled around on the ground, jabbing and scratching each other, his weight crushing me. I clawed at dirt and leaves, flinging what I could scrape into his face, but it was futile. What didn't reach his eyes sifted back down into mine. I flung my head from side to side, trying to grab something from my bag, but it was too far away.

I struggled and screeched, hoping my squirming would bump Ziggy off me. He might think he was the victim here, but I had news for him. Life hadn't been rosy for me since the perm-rod fiasco. I'd lost customers, self-esteem, and I'd felt more vulnerable to harm with every hour since his escape.

Somewhere in the pit of my stomach, a swarm of injustice erupted for the real victims. A murderer had taken Dooley's life. A murderer had stolen Jimmy's beloved cousin from him. Ziggy might not have been the one who'd pulled the trigger, but deep down I knew he was responsible. Not to mention I was about to lose my life if I didn't snap to action. I'd had enough of Ziggy Stoaks. I wasn't going to live under his curse anymore.

He slapped me across the face, and out of reflex, I slapped him back. Then I bit through his sling into his arm.

"*Ahhhhh!*" His eyes blazed with fury. "That's it! Take your last breath!" He squeezed my throat and gave my head another whack.

A thick fog surrounded my mind, and I was a beat away from spiraling into oblivion.

From a distance, I heard someone approaching, screaming like Tarzan swinging on a jungle vine.

The figure came up suddenly behind Ziggy and hurled white gunk on his head. Next thing I knew, a warped metal cage was rammed down on top of the white stuff and pushed down past his shoulders.

I blinked and forced myself to focus on my apparent hero.

Max!

A yeasty smell wafted my way, and I realized the goop Max had dumped on Ziggy was pizza dough. Buried underneath it, Ziggy tried to shriek, but all that came out was a muffled *fuff*.

He rolled off me, arms pinned to his sides. Trapped in the small cage, he struggled to his feet and staggered around in circles.

I gasped for air and scrambled away, too shaky to stand yet too alarmed to stay where I was.

Suddenly, we heard a soft gunshot, and Ziggy crashed backward, the cage rattling as it hit the ground.

I screamed in shock and looked around for the shooter, my mouth drooling from where I'd been slapped, my mind fighting to stay strong. Quivering all over, I gaped at my newfound hero, hoping he'd spring into action.

Max looked from Ziggy to me. His gaze rolled up to the top of his eyelids, and a second later, he fainted.

No!

I grabbed my bag and got my footing, a heightened fear rocking me. I was going to be targeted next. Before I could take another step, a silhouette came out of the woods.

I shook my head and wiped my eyes, focusing on the woman in a beige coat who looked vaguely familiar. She was holding a gun with a silencer on the end, and she had mousy brown hair and a forgettable face. Probably why I was having a hard time placing her.

She sneezed and rubbed her nose, then blinked several times like she had something in her eyes. Wouldn't have surprised me with all the dirt flying around. She took a deep breath and shuffled over until she was three feet away. The gun was firmly in hand, pointed at my chest.

"I should introduce myself." She sneezed again, and I noticed her eyes were red, irritated. "Gwen Scarpoli, M.D."

I was trying hard to concentrate on her words, but my mind was still foggy from the beating I'd taken, and I think I was in the throes of a panic attack because I'd lost track of my heartbeat.

"You're that troublesome hairdresser Ziggy was obsessed over."

I remained quiet, not certain where this was heading or what her M.D. stood for. Managing Director? Medical Doctor? Master's Postgraduate Degree? Or maybe she was a bartender, and this was code for More Drinks.

"I'm the physician who mended Ziggy after you maimed him with that ridiculous perm rod. I'm also the resident doctor at Rivers View."

Of course. The correctional center, yesterday. She was the woman in the white lab coat, standing at the wall behind Luther, seemingly uninterested in our conversation. Yet her brief remark to him showed she was more interested than she'd let on.

I tried not to look startled at placing her, but I doubted I was successful. I took a shallow breath, forcing myself to stay calm.

"Aha. So you recall seeing me during visitation yesterday." She leaned forward. "Think harder. Surely you remember seeing me again later."

I took a closer look at her face. *Hold on.* "I crashed into you at Kuruc's." When I was fleeing for the parking lot in search of my attacker. She must've left the prison after we'd vamoosed and followed us into town.

"Very good. I knew you were a sharp one."

A subtle whiff of hand cream floated by my nose, the same hand cream I'd used to fire at the maniac in Kuruc's. My gaze slid over to Ziggy, the so-called maniac. He was motionless on the ground, the bottom half of his London Fog sticking out from inside the cage. I swept my gaze back to Gwen. Um. Also in a London Fog. Were these matching His and Hers? Or was everyone getting deals lately on trench coats? I frowned. And Ziggy was at least twelve feet away. Why was I smelling my gingerbread-scented hand cream with him over there?

I was momentarily confused by this and searched my memory for what I could recall from the shooting. What stood out most was the high voice of my attacker. Ziggy's soprano voice.

Gwen wheezed, bringing me back to the present. "What the hell is that you're wearing? It's playing havoc with my allergies."

She sneezed for a third time, and suddenly it hit me. The gunman at Kuruc's sneezed at me from under the paper bag. That was right before I'd fired the hand cream. *Oh no!* Here I'd been pinning the shooting on Ziggy, not only because of the high-pitched voice, but because I'd wanted to believe it was him. But it was Gwen! "You were the shooter!"

My heart leaped to my throat, and alarm bells clanged in my ears. I tried not to fix my stare on the gun in her hand, silencer and all. But it was identical to the one that had been aimed at me at Kuruc's. It had to be the same gun.

I expected her to make another wisecrack about my snappy intellect, but she was too busy sniffling and rubbing her nose. This gave me time to figure things out.

Gwen must've dodged out of the deli, pocketed the gun, thrown the crumpled bag in the Dumpster, and returned to the front in time to see me exit the front door.

Since onlookers had started gathering, I hadn't noticed what she'd worn when I'd bumped into her. But it had to be the trench coat. She'd taken a chance I wouldn't spot it. And she was right. "Why'd you do it?" I asked. "Why target me in a store?"

She rolled her eyes. "You're a hard one to pin down. Flitting from one place to another. You think it was easy for me to enter that deli and threaten you?"

Inside, I was hyperventilating, and my heart felt like it was going to break out of my chest. On the outside, I fought to appear in control. "You seemed pretty sure of yourself."

"What I was sure of was that you'd thought it was Ziggy. Guess I was right."

She took a long, arduous sniff. "Bad enough I choked on that hand cream of yours, but your perfume is more than I can take. What do you do, bathe in the stuff?"

I did, because I loved the scent, but I kept that to myself. "Maybe I should step back so it doesn't bother you."

She waved the gun in my face. "Stay right where you are."

Her voice was strong, but she was distracted by her runny nose and inflamed eyes. She squeezed her eyes shut for a second, sighed in exasperation, then centered on me again. "Ziggy never would've escaped if it hadn't been for my help. We'd become rather…close and were going to run away together. If only the dolt hadn't become fixated on killing Dooley and hunting you down." She scowled at Ziggy's still body. "Once he was free, he told me to get lost. Said he didn't need me anymore."

"Men." I wasn't trying to buddy up to her, but I knew the feelings she was experiencing.

"Yeah. Right? While he was tracing *you*, I was trailing *him*." She leered down at him. "Jackass. He didn't realize I was one step ahead of him."

I heard her words, but I struggled to understand what she meant by them.

She pulled out a tissue and blew her nose. Meanwhile, I pleaded with God to help me put the pieces together, help me discover a window into Gwen's mind.

Suddenly, I recalled my conversation with Dom at Lumber Mart. He'd seen a white car rolling down my street yesterday morning. A white car with a logo on the door. A plumber, he'd thought, or an electrician.

I squinted at Gwen, adding this up. I bet anything she was the woman driving the car, and the car belonged to Rivers View Correctional Center. Their logo was water flowing through jail bars. I'd seen it myself yesterday when we'd arrived at the prison gate.

Dom connecting water and bars to a plumber had merit. The electrician connection was less clear. But electricians worked with wire, and the prison was surrounded with barbed wire fencing. It was a bit of a leap, but the mind did funny things when looking for answers.

I hugged my bag to my side, things finally starting to click. "You were the one who placed that dildo on my porch." Ziggy had told the truth. He'd never touched that apparatus.

She nodded, stuffing the tissue in her pocket. "Complete with perm rod, don't forget. Exactly how I'd found it snaked around Ziggy's scrotum."

Seemed I wasn't the only person who'd been up close and personal with Ziggy's bangers.

"I drove down your street several times after coming to your door. Didn't want any critters looking for *nuts* to scamper away with the goods."

She grinned at her joke, then glared back at Ziggy. "If the fool wanted to ditch me, why not plant something that would incriminate him? If nothing else, a dildo on your porch after Ziggy's escape would do the job and grab that sexy cop's attention."

This was true. We'd all thought Ziggy was the sender of the dildo. There was nothing concrete to believe anything else. The sexy-cop remark had me puzzled, though.

"You know Romero?"

She gave a slight shrug. "Cops aren't strangers to prisons. Plus, Ziggy had told me stuff that Dooley had shared when he'd been following you. We'd even laughed about his clever plan to get revenge on you. When he mentioned Romero's name, I knew I'd seen the detective at Norfolt before."

My heart was pummeling in my chest, and a sick feeling churned in my stomach. But I had to ask the next question.

"Why did you kill Dooley?"

Her nose had started running again, and she gave it an angry swipe. "I went in search of Dooley after Ziggy's escape. Since Ziggy had dumped me, I was hoping Dooley would know where to find him. But the little guy said he knew nothing. He even threatened to go to the police if we hurt you."

She gave an insane laugh. "Can you believe some people? He had no weapon, no muscle, yet he thought he could scare me with his measly threat."

Pieces of her hair had fallen into her eyes from laughing. She raked the ends behind her ear and gestured back at Ziggy. "If the dildo delivery wasn't enough to incriminate that rotten fink, Dooley's murder was."

Poor Dooley. Seemed like everyone wanted him dead.

Her gaze became fixed on her gun. "Two-Notes may have arranged a weapon for Ziggy, but I keep this baby in my car." She muttered with venom in her voice. "You'd think working in a prison you'd feel safe. Ha!"

She darted another vile look at Ziggy lying motionless on the ground. A lone tear seeped onto her bottom lid. It clung there fiercely as if it refused to roll down her cheek, refused to give credence that she'd cared for Ziggy. "Now that it's all in the open, I need to say goodbye to this buffoon."

Her voice turned remorseful. "Sadly, I'll have to kill all three of you in the process. But I can't afford to let Ziggy live. He's too much of a threat. And your death, well, would seem the reason he's dead. Don't worry. I'll make it look like you all got shot fighting over Ziggy's gun."

Worry! I was way beyond worried.

She scratched her head miserably, swinging her gaze from Ziggy to Max to me. "It's the best idea. Only, the story will go that the sorry bastard lost his gun and stole mine from my car. His rampage started with murdering Dooley, then continued at Kuruc's, and ended with all three of you being killed. Don't you love when a plan comes together?"

The sick feeling in my stomach rose to my throat. This unassuming doctor who'd made the mistake of getting involved with a convict was going to end my life. And Max's. This was it. I was about to meet my maker.

Max was out cold, and a sprout of blood trickled from under Ziggy and the cage.

I bent over to cough, the pain in my throat from being choked taking a backseat to the terror before me. *Stay with it, Valentine. You can't lose consciousness.* The forest swayed in and out, and my head felt woozy, but I had to do *something*. Max had just saved my life. It was my turn to save his.

Think, for Pete's sake. You're a beautician. Use it!

Right. I straightened and mopped a mix of sweat and dirt off my forehead with my scarf. *Here goes nothing.*

"You could walk away and start a new life." I treaded slowly, stuffing down the queasiness. "You don't need Ziggy. You're a beautiful woman. Surely, you have other love interests."

Her dreary eyes popped open. "Me? Beautiful? The only reason Ziggy was interested in me was because he'd been planning this escape for a long time. I see that now. He knew I was his ticket out." She tightened her thin, unadorned lips. "I could've lost my job over that son-of-a-bitch."

I winced at her hateful words toward Ziggy. "Let me help you. I could give you a makeover, and you could start fresh."

"A makeover? For me? I don't know. I'm so plain. My name should've been Jane. Dr. Plain Jane." She lowered her gun. "My nose is pointy. My eyes are beady." She tugged at her stringy hair. "And this is the best my hair has ever looked, and you can see how bad *that* is."

I pulled my own hair from my wrecked bun off my forehead. "You're not so plain, and everyone has at least *one* beautiful feature."

Everything went silent around us as she gazed into my eyes, brows raised like she'd never considered this before. "Really? What's *my* one beautiful feature?"

I was afraid she was going to ask this. I studied her hard, giving her a hopeful smile. "Your eyes are…and your nose is…and your hair has…" Oh boy. How much time did I have before she shot me dead?

Wait! An idea hit me. "It all starts with good posture."

"Huh?"

"You know. You've got to walk the walk." I didn't know where I was going with this, but I had her attention, so I kept prattling. "When you came out of that forest, you were hunched over, dragging your feet, like the world was sitting on your shoulders."

She glanced at the forest and back at me. "It *has* felt like I've been under a lot of pressure lately."

"See? You're a respected doctor. What kind of professional skulks around with her head down? You need to walk with purpose. Head up, shoulders back. Like you own it."

"Like I own it." She stared pensively into space.

"Yes! That attitude will go much further than a mere makeover. A woman walking with purpose is more attractive than someone shuffling around, staring at her navel. Let me show you what I mean."

I fixed my bun, flung my scarf out of my way, and despite the pain racking my body, I sashayed forward like I was on the Paris catwalk. Then I did a beautiful pivot, not sure how my legs were supporting me when they were quaking in my boots. "Your turn. Keep your head high, shoulders back, bum tucked under."

She bit her lip, counted silently on her fingers, then

took a deep breath, and stomped toward me like a Patriots offensive lineman.

Good grief.

"That's it! You're a natural." A wee fib never hurt anyone. And if she wasn't fixed on killing me, I'd have helped her perfect her walk.

I rooted around in my bag, ignoring my heartbeat that was booming in my ears. "I've got just the thing that will improve that strut."

Interested, she leaned in, stretching her neck to see what I had.

"Aha! Found it." I elbowed her in the throat, whipped out my perfume, and sprayed it in her face.

"*Aaaaah!*" She dropped the gun, falling knees to the ground, clawing at her eyes. "It's burning! I can't see!"

It was a dirty trick, but I wasn't here to make friends with Dr. Plain Jane. I trussed her up with my scarf like a Christmas turkey. Then I scrounged in my bag for a water and, out of pity, poured a dab in each of her eyes. She whimpered a thank-you and hung her head in shame.

In the distance, I heard sirens peal. I calmed my beating heart and kicked the gun at my feet in Max's direction, grazing his hand.

"Aah!" He squealed so high I thought the voice was coming from Ziggy.

My eyes widened. "You were awake?"

"Someone had to call the cops!" He sat up. "You did such a fine job with the beauty advice, she didn't even notice me. Bravo!"

I smiled at Max, suddenly recalling the first homicide I'd stumbled onto. I'd been inexperienced, incompetent, and scared of my own shadow. Now look at me. I was standing over a murderer whom I'd apprehended with a beauty product and my own scarf. I felt triumphant and a little bit pleased. I would've feigned a fists-on-hips Wonder-Woman pose, but I settled for glancing back at Gwen and taking a long, satisfied breath. I *had* done a fine job. And Romero wasn't even here to see me in action.

Chapter 18

Huge snowflakes landed gently on the ground, making a pretty picture outside while I zipped up my boots and pulled on my coat. It was Saturday, five days since the cops had resuscitated Ziggy and hauled Gwen Scarpoli away. Like it or not, they were both going to spend a long time behind bars.

I still felt jittery in public places and jumped at loud noises—more so than usual. And I still expected to greet a grotesque gadget on my porch when I left the house. My scrapes and bruises had faded, but the horrible memories and emotional wounds were a different matter. Past involvement in murder cases told me those would take time to heal. More than anything, I was grateful to be alive, knowing this nightmare was over.

Things slowly returned to normal at work. Phyllis proudly displayed her completed-course certificate on the wall by her station, and Max took pains to restrain himself from bringing up Austin's strange appearance at Friar Tuck's.

I grinned, recalling Max's bravery in my time of need, and his quick thinking using the pizza dough. In the end, his bread machine had been a godsend. Sure, Max wasn't Tarzan, or even Robin, though he'd probably rock the tights. Still, he was the best male friend a girl could have, and that was something I'd never forget.

Jock cornered me in my office the first day back and told me that now that Stoaks and the doctor were locked away for good, life was only going to get better. Not sure what he meant by that, I tilted my gaze up from his taut chest muscles, straining through his shirt, for the answer in his deep, compelling eyes.

He touched my jaw, his fingers lingering at the base of my hairline. "Speaking of life getting better…" His voice was low, smooth. "Know what I'm learning to love about you?"

I swallowed thickly, not trusting myself to move. I stared steadfastly into his cognac-colored eyes, melting from the hypnotic impact. "Do I really want to know?"

He brought me closer, cupping his hands around my face. All humor vanished from his eyes. "You stay true to yourself. You may be impulsive and headstrong, but I like a woman who knows who she is."

My legs weakened, and my insides fluttered. Jock had a knack for making a woman feel beautiful, confident, and secure, even if she was an impulsive, headstrong wreck.

One thing I'd learned this past week was that he was a man I wanted in my life. I didn't know in what context, and maybe I'd never know. But for now, I'd cherish what I had with this stunt-doubling, ex-navy master-at-arms. In a word, *Hercules*.

He'd pressed a kiss onto my forehead and, as was Jock's style, left me wanting more.

I told Yitts I wouldn't be late, then locked up, and headed to the Wee Irish Dude. I had a date with a tall Italian stud.

By the time I stepped into the busy restaurant, the snowfall had stopped and the temperature had risen. Perfect night for a grand opening. An Irish tune, boasting a flute, a fiddle, and a banjo, played merrily in the background. And sparkly green shamrocks—the sparkle being my idea—added a little *je ne sais quoi* to the walls and staircase.

Beer flowed heavily from the wooden kegs on the bar, and a blend of smells from lamb stew, to corned beef and cabbage, to burgers and fries filled the air. Great, because I was starving, and something with a hint of garlic was making my mouth water.

I'd taken extra care tonight with my clothes and appearance. I hadn't seen Romero since the case had ended, and I wasn't sure where we stood. He'd been the first on the scene at the puppy mill and had wasted no time cuffing Gwen and saving Ziggy from suffocating to death. Our moment there together had been brief, but the look in his eyes had said there'd be words later.

We'd agreed to meet at the restaurant since he thought he'd be working late. But when I shrugged off my coat and straightened my figure-hugging dress in the foyer mirror, I noticed he was already sitting at a table in a black tight-knit shirt with a beer in front of him, eyeing me up like I was a tasty Irish Cream.

I waded through the crowd and slid onto my chair. "Whew! Who would've thought Jimmy's first night would be such a success?"

I stuffed my coat behind me and was so busy looking around that it took me a second to note Romero hadn't said a word. My heart skipped a beat, and my core trembled. Fear of the unknown, I told myself. I swiveled my legs forward and forced myself to face his intimate stare.

His beard had grown since the case had begun, and it added a new dimension to his dangerous, sexy appearance. That, mixed with the passion in his eyes, engulfed me, and suddenly it was as if the music and chatter had stopped, and we were alone in a bubble.

My cheeks heated, and my lower parts tingled with anticipation. How could one man make a woman feel so desired in a roomful of people? Romero did that without even trying.

An attractive woman at the bar in a low-cut top batted her eyelashes at Romero, hoping to catch his attention. At one time, he might've given her a nod. But tonight, his focus was totally on me.

I returned his gaze cautiously, a hesitant notion warning me the passion in his eyes might not be from adoration. What if it was anger, and he was about to explode? *Yikes*. I needed to say something before he—or I—burst.

Suppressing the queasiness in my stomach, I worked up my nerve, offering the first thing that popped to mind. "Nice weather we're having."

He raised an eyebrow at the entrance where a couple stomped in from the cold, *brrr*-ing and dusting snow off their coats. Then he tilted his head back at me.

"It wasn't snowing a minute ago." I paused at the blank look on his face. "And the temperature must've dropped."

No reaction.

I pushed down a swallow. Might as well get it over with. "Go ahead."

"Go ahead?" His tone was deep, sensual.

"Yes. Aren't you going to yell at me for ignoring your request to stay away from the puppy mill?"

"No." He studied me in his predatory way that told me he liked when I was unsure of his mood.

"What about when I called you pig-headed?" I ducked, thinking this might set him off.

He shook his head. "Nope."

I straightened. "Are you mad at all?"

"Mad? Mad doesn't cover the emotions I'm feeling right now."

I blinked down at my hands, scrunching my fingers into balls, waiting for the inevitable. Suddenly, I'd lost my appetite. I mean, this had to be it. He was done with me.

He reached across the table and lifted my chin. "I'm trying to understand how one person can get herself into so much trouble in one day." He looked at the wooden barrels lining the stairs, then dragged his gaze back to me.

"You find a dead body in a beer keg, discover a sex toy on your doorstep, then you cause me extra grief by trekking to a prison to question inmates. And *that* was all before noon." His voice rose a decibel, and a couple at another table gave us a guarded look.

I fidgeted with my hands on my lap. "Actually, it was *after* lunch when we visited Luther." I winced, doubting my next comment would help things either. "And I only questioned one inmate."

"My mistake." He rubbed his beard like he was considering his next words. "I probably don't need to express my thoughts on the Kuruc's episode or the chopper mishap. Again, all in the same day."

I squirmed in my chair, focusing on the wooden ceiling fans, circling 'round and 'round, absently thinking about Ziggy flying off the propellers into Neverland. "Nope. I have a pretty good idea what your thoughts are."

"Good. Just so we're clear."

My gaze dropped back to his face. "That's it? You're not going to holler or wave your arms in the air…or swear in Italian?"

"What good would it do?"

True. I peered into his eyes with the bigger question. "Are you ending it?"

"Ending it?" Was it my imagination, or was there a roguish gleam in the corner of his eye? "Is that what you thought?"

I drummed the tabletop nervously. "Maybe?"

He extended his arms across the table and curved his large, strong hands over mine. The warmth from his grasp and the way he stroked my skin calmed me and, at the same time, sent electrifying jolts to my pelvis.

He took a deep breath, then blew out air. "You're impossible to stay mad at. And the truth is, despite all your meddling…despite how many times I had to scold you… despite—"

I erupted impatiently. "Could you get past your spite and tell me what the truth is?"

He grinned at my cheekiness. "You were so busy tracking Stoaks, it made it easier for the police to concentrate on Scarpoli."

"Glad I could be such a help." I sniffed, fighting to keep my tone sweet.

His smile waned. "We knew Scarpoli was involved in the case. We just weren't sure to what degree. Further investigation at the prison revealed private meetings and conversations between the two before Stoaks escaped."

He paused, and I tried to read the look that crossed his face. It wasn't exactly lighthearted, but it wasn't serious either. "Then there were his phone records, which weren't easy to find. Looked like someone tried to cover up the calls." He leaned in and gave my hands a playful squeeze. "By the way, thanks for the tip to search our boy's files. But fascinatingly enough, sometimes we detectives think of these things for ourselves."

I gave him a prim look. "Well, it never hurts to get assistance on the matter." I tried to remain uppity, but it was useless. He granted me one of his sexy, macho winks, and instantly I felt stripped in more ways than one.

"And finally," he said, "when forensics couldn't get a match on Stoaks from the saliva on the paper bag, we knew we had to act fast to catch the real shooter."

He took a swig of his beer and sat back comfortably. "We moved Scarpoli to another jail tonight. I wanted to be there to make sure the transition went smoothly, but everything went according to plan, and I got here earlier than expected." He wiped his mouth with the back of his hand, his brows creasing in concern at me. "How are the bruises?"

"Better, thank you." I tried to sound carefree. "Didn't you see me cartwheel coming in?"

The corner of his mouth slid up a fraction of an inch. "And on the inside?"

I gave a slight shrug. "In all honesty, going back to work helped in finding normalcy." There was nothing normal about Beaumont's or the people working there, but it was what I had, and I'd keep it.

He nodded, his face tough as ever, but his eyes softened in a way I'd seen before. "Not that I'm condoning your actions heading out to the puppy mill on your own, but I've got to hand it to you, you saved the day. That underground shelter Stoaks and Boyle had made was well hidden *and* well camouflaged. No wonder my men thought the place was abandoned. Congratulations on the discovery."

I didn't see the point in bringing up the fact that Max and I'd placed our bets on the building being Ziggy's hideout and the roof being his entrance. I was too busy feeling triumphant.

"What's more," he said, "Scarpoli was the sweetest-smelling perp I've ever known. A nice change from the reeking scum I lock up every day."

I blushed at the reference to my Musk, then thought about Max and the pizza dough. "I did have help with the capture, but I'm flattered you're pleased."

He gave me a grim look that all but wiped my smugness away. "You wear my patience thin, and just when I think I've got you figured out, you do something that shocks me and sends my tail spinning."

Before I could defend myself with a list of my worthier traits, he raised his palm to stop me. "But I'm learning to appreciate things I have control over and accept things I don't." He shook his head in resignation. "And one thing I'm discovering about you is that nothing I say or do will restrain you when you've got your mind set."

"You could *try* to restrain me," I peeped, uncomfortable with his assessment, not sure if he was playing with me.

"What would be the point? You'd flip out, make a scene, and probably get injured in the process."

Now I *knew* he was playing with me. "You're right. I'm stubborn. Impetuous. Determined. *And a Type A*. And if you don't like those things, well…it's who I am."

He gave me another thick-lashed wink, and my heart soared in my chest. "I'm beginning to know who you are. I don't want you to change. And if you do, I'll tie you up until you beg me to release you."

Whew. All this tension and emotion and heat were arousing me, in an Irish pub, no less, with a hundred people surrounding me. I grabbed my napkin and fanned myself, bringing a low chuckle from Romero.

He extended his arm in the air, getting Jimmy's attention from the other side of the room. Another of Romero's gifts. He raised his hand, and people came running.

"Hey, dudette!" Jimmy chirped in his green Celtics jersey, sliding his scrawny butt onto the empty chair between Romero and me. "Pretty righteous night, don't you think?" He waggled his bushy black eyebrows a foot from my face.

"It most definitely is." I avoided Romero's fiery stare sizzling through me and smiled at Jimmy, a sense of relief hitting me again at how much he loved his new look.

"And I got you, Jock, Max, Phyllis...and this big guy here to thank." He did a fist pump on Romero's toned shoulder, then winced and rubbed his knuckles from hitting Romero's wall of muscle.

My staff and I had all helped Jimmy prepare for this day, and I'd finished assisting him last night with the final decorations. But where did Romero come into play?

"Like your crime-squad dude saw to it that I had a full cooking staff in place. I mean, whoa, there's no way I could've managed that on my own this week, especially with the way things transpired."

Romero had come to the Skink's rescue? Helping someone who'd earned a living scalping tickets? Someone who was related to a convicted felon? The respect and admiration I had for Romero leaped a couple of notches, but before he saw the delight in my eyes, I centered on Jimmy. "He's pretty amazing, isn't he?"

"I'll say." He lowered his head for a moment and sniffed. "Like Dools would've loved this."

I leaned over and patted Jimmy's hand. "No question about it."

He wiped his eye and bobbed his head up, his blond curls springing all over his head. "Come on." He grabbed my arm and pulled me away from the table. "I've got to show you this."

I shrugged at Romero as I was being dragged away, and he gave me a wave that said *enjoy*.

Jimmy and I bounced into the kitchen, the trail of garlic I'd smelled earlier ending here. Now I knew why.

I stood there, gaping from my mother to Tantig, wearing chef's hats and white aprons, placing hot shish kebab on plates with sides of grape leaves and hummus. "Mom?"

"Surprise, dear!" She passed the loaded plates to a couple of servers. Then she tossed a spoon to one of the other four cooks, who looked suspiciously like one of the cops I'd seen before at the police station, and who was obviously enjoying working in tandem with my mother and great-aunt.

I gawked open-mouthed at the action in the kitchen. Bowls clanging. Pots boiling. Cooks hustling. Before I could utter a word, Max strolled out of the walk-in fridge with his own chef's hat perched on his head, carrying two pizzas ready for the oven.

"Max?" I blinked wide-eyed, spotting his bread machine on the far counter.

"Lovey!" he called over the din.

I gaped from Max to my mother. "What's going on?"

She wiped her hands on her apron. "Romero asked if we'd help out in the kitchen until Jimmy was on his feet, and we thought why not? My time is my own, and you know how Tantig loves to cook. It's given her a purpose."

"Uh…and Dad?"

She gave a glib wave. "He's in heaven, eating everything on the menu."

My gaze swiveled to Tantig. "Isn't this too much for her?"

Tantig gave me her disinterested look, her monotone voice competing with the clatter in the kitchen. "I told them they needed *kay*-bob on the menu, and that kid with the curly hair said he'd add it as a featured dish."

Jimmy howled with laughter. "Like did I ever, Tiggy-mama. It's so popular, I might have to keep it on the menu." He plucked a piece of lamb off a skewer and stuffed it in his mouth. "Like *far out!*"

I looked at Max again, trying to establish a time and place Romero had lined all this up. Why bother? It didn't involve me, and everything seemed to be running smoothly.

"You see?" my mother chimed. "A win-win for—"

Suddenly, there was a *crash*. We all spun our heads to the back door where Phyllis had bustled in, arms full of clean dishrags. She'd knocked a dishwasher on his ass, taking with him a stack of plates.

"—almost everyone," my mother finished, rolling her eyes at the mess.

She poked her head outside the kitchen door. "Look at your father at the bar, wearing that ridiculous leprechaun hat, joking it up with everyone. He's having more fun than watching Bruce Willis in those silly action movies every night."

I twisted around and spotted my father doing a jig around a beer barrel. Go figure.

The wooden keg had me thinking again about Dooley and all that had happened in a few short days. Though his life had ended too soon, his character had been restored, and he could rest in peace now that his killer had been caught.

Jimmy had held a small service yesterday afternoon in Dooley's honor and even had a picture of him hanging over the bar. A short inscription beneath read: *Dooley, the greatest cousin there ever was.*

I wiped a tear from my eye and ambled back to the table. "Wonders never cease." I plunked myself down in my seat and stared at a glass of something fruity that had appeared in my absence. "What's this?" I looked from the tall drink with a pink umbrella piercing an orange slice on top to Romero.

"I ordered it for you. A Shirley Temple."

"Thank you." I took a hearty sip of the sweet, tangy drink and gazed back at this handsome, noble Iron Man sitting across from me. "And thank you for helping the Skink."

"It was nothing." He shrugged it off like it was no big deal. "Just a few phone calls."

"It was a grand idea, and I adore you for thinking of it. It's like a well-oiled machine in there." With one exception. Then again, the fact that Phyllis was helping someone else showed she didn't have ice in her veins. Perhaps there was hope for her after all.

A sense of well-being filled me inside. Maybe Jimmy wouldn't have Dooley to help run the restaurant, and maybe life for him felt low right now, but he'd be okay. If nothing else, Jimmy was resilient. He'd come from modest beginnings, scraped his way scalping tickets, and was now sole owner of the Wee Irish Dude. For someone who'd once told me working was the pits, he'd developed a strong work ethic, and I was even more confident this place would be a success.

Romero felt in his jacket pocket behind him. "Now that the case is over…" He pulled out my gingerbread-scented hand cream that he'd confiscated the day of the shooting. "This is yours, I believe."

He slanted over the table, moved my drink out of reaching distance, and drew my right arm toward him. His rugged appearance was melting me, and his sexy gesture stirred me.

As usual, I was full of questions. "What are you—?"

He put his finger to my lips to silence me, then slid his hand up my sleeve until my inner arm was exposed. Next, he flicked open the lid on the cream, his eyes not leaving mine. Without a word, he placed the nozzle on my wrist and squeezed a line of cream straight across.

The rich emollient tickled my skin, and it was torture having my arm pinned down with Romero staring into my soul.

"I…" He studied me, his expression serious.

My hands trembled, my impatience getting the best of me.

He knew the effect he was having on me, and he was loving it. His striking blue eyes twinkled like there was nothing in the world that could drag him away from this. Mutely, he took the tube of cream and squeezed out a *C*.

By now, nearby diners were ogling us, whispering and nodding, wondering what Romero would write next. My heart thumped wildly. *I* wanted to know what Romero would write next.

The *C* was followed by a *U*.

"I *see U*?" Jimmy landed on the spare chair out of nowhere, his nose an inch from my arm. "Like, whoa, dude. That's majorly cryptic."

Romero gave Jimmy a devilish grin, then squeezed a backward *C* that joined the other. With his finger, he swiped the bottoms of the C's down until they came to a point.

I blinked at my arm. It wasn't a *C* at all. It was a heart.

Jimmy bolted up on his chair, his spindly arms flailing in the air. "He hearts her! Whoa! Like riiiiighteous!" He waved to the crowd. "Drinks on the house!"

Everyone was cheering and applauding, and again it was as if I were in a bubble with this gorgeous hero. A cop. A leader. A tough, hard-headed man who spent his life devoted to capturing criminals. A man who had won my affection.

"You heart me?" I said softly, the noise in the background playing in the distance.

"Undeniably. Uncontrollably." He got to his feet, pulled me off my chair, and framed my face in his hands. "Unequivocally."

Not bothered that the place was full of onlookers, he gently stroked my bottom lip with his thumb, then closed the gap between us, and pressed a gentle kiss on my lips.

He stole a look up at Jimmy entertaining the crowd, tapping his own Irish jig atop the chair seat. Romero shook his head in amusement and dropped his gaze back to me, his face, without question, full of adoration. "For once, it's nice to know *you're* not the one making a scene."

I tamed the powerful rush from his kiss charging through my body and moved in until my mouth was an inch from his ear. "Don't underestimate my abilities." I gave his ear lobe a playful lick and felt his breath catch in his throat. "Nobody knows what tomorrow may bring."

BOOK 1

MURDER, CURLERS, AND CREAM

Valentine Beaumont is a beautician with a problem. Not only has she got a meddling mother, a wacky staff, and a dying business, but now she's got a dead client who was strangled while awaiting her facial.

With business the way it is, combing through this mystery may be the only way to save her salon. Until a second murder, an explosion, a kidnapping, death threats, and the hard-nosed Detective Romero complicate things. But Valentine will do anything to untangle the crime. That's if she can keep her tools of the trade in her bag, keep herself alive, and avoid falling for the tough detective.

In the end, how hard can that be?

BOOK 2

MURDER, CURLERS, AND CANES

Valentine Beaumont is back in her second hair-raising mystery, this time, trying to find out who had it in for an elderly nun. Only trouble is there are others standing in her way: hot but tough Detective Romero, sexy new stylist Jock de Marco, and some zany locals who all have a theory on the nun's death.

Making things worse: the dead nun's secret that haunts Valentine, another murder, car chases, death threats, mysterious clues, an interfering mother, and a crazy staff.

Between brushing off Jock's advances and splitting hairs with handsome Detective Romero, Valentine struggles to comb through the crime, utilizing her tools of the trade in some outrageous situations. Question is, will she succeed?

BOOK 3

MURDER, CURLERS, AND CRUISES

In her third fast-paced mystery, beautician Valentine Beaumont and her madcap crew sail the high seas on a Caribbean "Beauty Cruise." When a bizarre murder takes place onboard, Valentine finds herself swept into the middle of the investigation.

If things aren't bad enough, her mother is playing matchmaker, a loved one is kidnapped, drug smuggling is afoot, a hair contest proves disastrous, and a strange alliance between tough Detective Romero and sexy stylist Jock de Marco rubs Valentine the wrong way.

Will this impulsive beauty sleuth comb through the catastrophes and untangle the mystery, or will this voyage turn into another fatal Titanic? With Jock and Romero onboard, it's destined to be a hot cruise!

What's Next in
The Valentine Beaumont Mysteries

MURDER, CURLERS, AND KILTS
A Valentine Beaumont Mini Mystery

MURDER, CURLERS, AND KITES
A Valentine Beaumont Mini Mystery

Book Club Discussion Questions

Enjoy the banter while you share these questions with your book club!

1. The story opens in an Irish pub. Is there a themed bar or restaurant you frequent?

2. Jimmy the Skink gets a new look when he lets Phyllis tint his eyebrows and eyelashes. Have you ever had a new look that was borderline bizarre?

3. Dooley closely resembled his cousin Jimmy. Do you have any relatives whom you look like?

4. Max's guilty pleasure is anything made from a bread machine. What's your guilty pleasure?

5. Valentine gets the ride of her life, touring Boston in a unique way. What's the most unique mode of transportation you've used for touring a city?

6. Once again, Valentine wields her beauty tools for protection. Name 2 things you carry in your bag that you could use to defend yourself if you were ever attacked.

7. Ziggy is known for having a high-pitched voice. What are some distinct characteristics about yourself?

8. Valentine shops for international foods at Kuruc's European Deli. Is there a grocery store you visit for ethnic foods?

9. Did you have any idea who the murderer was?

10. Team Jock or Team Romero?

Note to Readers

Thank you for taking the time to read MURDER, CURLERS, AND KEGS. If you enjoyed Valentine's story, please consider telling your friends or posting a short review. Word of mouth is an author's best friend and much appreciated. Thank you!

Social Media Links

Website: www.arlenemcfarlane.com

Newsletter Sign-up:
www.arlenemcfarlane.com/signup/signup5.html

Facebook: facebook.com/ArleneMcFarlaneAuthor/

Facebook Readers' Group:
www.facebook.com/groups/1253793228097364/

Twitter: @mcfa_arlene

Pinterest: pinterest.com/amcfarlane0990

Arlene McFarlane is the *USA Today* bestselling author of the *Murder, Curlers* series. Previously an aesthetician, hairstylist, and owner of a full-service salon, Arlene now writes full time. When she's not making up stories, or being a wife, mother, daughter, sister, friend, cat-mom, or makeover artist, you'll find her making music on the piano.

Arlene is a member of Romance Writers of America, Sisters in Crime, Toronto Romance Writers, SOWG, and the Golden Network. She's won and placed in over 30 contests, including twice in the Golden Heart and twice in the Daphne du Maurier.

Arlene lives with her family in Canada.

www.arlenemcfarlane.com